I0625965

Not Just Another Interlude

LARA T. KAREEM

Lara T Kareem

First Published in Great Britain in 2020 by
LOVE AFRICA PRESS
103 Reaver House, 12 East Street, Epsom KT17 1HX
www.loveafricapress.com

Text copyright © Lara T Kareem, 2020

All rights reserved.
No part of this publication may be reproduced, stored or
transmitted in any form by any means, electronic, mechanical,
photocopying or otherwise, without the prior permission of the
publisher, except in the case of brief quotations embodied in
reviews.

The right of Lara T Kareem to be identified as author of
this work has been asserted by them in accordance with the
Copyright, Design and Patents Act, 1988

This is a work of fiction. Names, places, events and
incidents are either the products of the author's imagination or
used fictitiously. Any resemblance to actual persons, living or
dead, is purely coincidental.

ISBN: 978-1-9163628-7-1
Also available as ebook

DEDICATION

To the ladies fighting against patriarchy in their own little ways.

Lara T Kareem

ACKNOWLEDGEMENTS

Dear Tosin, Stephanie, Chisom & Tembi when I think of my writing journey, you four play an important role, because you ladies were always cheering me on, eagerly reading my stories and always asking for the next chapter or story. I am grateful and thankful for you, because without your encouragements I may have given up on writing.

Thank you to my wonderful Salewa, Dami & Ivie, you ladies are the best support system and I am so lucky to have you in my corner cheering the loudest for all that I do.

Thank you Math & Adaeze, your input when it came to editing and putting together this book means more than you'll ever know.

Thank you to my Aunt Petty, who found one of my stories in a notebook and got my mum to support my writing hobby and my family members for supporting my bookworm tendencies.

Thank you for the love and support to all my Bookstagram & Literary friends, there are so many of you I can't even begin to name you all (so I don't miss out anyone's name)

Thank you to my editor Zee for polishing up this story into its final glory and Kiru Taye for making one of my lifelong dreams a reality.

Finally, I have to thank you, the reader. This is for you.

CHAPTER ONE

I wonder what would happen if I threw caution to the wind—damn the consequences and the domino effect it could have on my life. If I walked up to him and told him straight, "I want you to be my future."

I'm exaggerating a bit—the worst that could happen is he flat-out says no and proceeds to end whatever it is that we have but haven't entirely defined or named.

I would run away if someone I'd known for less than a month comes up to me and makes such a declaration—although I wouldn't if it was him, though. I'm way in over my head when it comes to him. It's like Cupid shot an arrow that hit me on my right butt cheek from the moment my gaze fell upon him. And when he spoke to me, I knew it was a match made in Heaven.

Love-struck. That's how I describe myself ever since that day. Nothing else comes close to explaining how I feel, so it has to do, and I have an inkling he feels the same way, or else I'm going to dig a massive hole in a forest and pay someone without a heart to bury me alive.

To hell with it. I'm doing it. After a quick trip to the ladies' to make sure I look good and embody a woman who is sure of herself, confident and exuberant, I walk out of there like I own the place and immediately slam into a body.

It's not pretty: I lose my footings and fall right on my ass, and I may not or may have screamed as I went down. Is God trying to send me a message?

"Do you need a hand?"

I look up at the human brick that has me ass-sitting on the floor of a restaurant, and that's when I realise that I am still down on that hard surface. I take the hand he has stretched out, and he helps by pulling me up.

I'm dying of embarrassment now. I can feel people's eyes on me and glance around to see several people looking at me with smiles on their faces while some seem sorry for me, and some just shake their heads before returning their focus to the reason why they'd come to this restaurant in the first place.

"Thanks, I'm such a klutz," I say, taking a full look at my human brick.

Whoa, it can't be just me feeling the effect of looking at his face, because the room suddenly seems ten times brighter and hotter than it was seconds ago.

He is beautiful. Oh, gosh, I am staring. A blush creeps up at the smile that is taking over his face; my staring is that obvious.

"No problem. I wasn't exactly paying attention to my surroundings. So I didn't notice the door had opened, but I'm not sorry a beautiful woman walked into me. Is your derrière okay?"

Excuse me? Did I hear him right? Can the world just let me melt into a puddle of embarrassment? His voice is entrancing, deep, but delivers softly, like a caress, and of course, he's a flirt. The beautiful ones usually are. He is flirting, right? Or is that his way of being polite? Either way, I know my cheeks are at full puff because I can't help but shyly smile at the compliment he blessed me with.

"Sewa?"

I look back, and Lucas is steadily approaching me. I smile at him and turn back to the beautiful stranger, who smiles at me, dips his head in farewell, and walks off. My full attention stays on the fine male specimen walking away from me, before returning to Lucas. I smile again when he's finally by my side and go in for a hug. He hugs me back but releases me almost instantly, to my disappointment.

"Who was that?"

"You missed the show, Lu. I collided with him and fell ass to the floor."

"That would have been spectacular to watch," he says before bursting into laughter.

Of course he would laugh. I don't feel bad because I would do the same if he ends up in an embarrassing situation. I roll my eyes, and he smiles at me before putting his arm around my shoulder and leading us to a table.

Once we chose a secluded spot for two, a waiter approaches us with the menu. Trepidation settles in my bones like a million little jolts. I'm not going to back out now, because I have decided to just do it. If I don't take risks, I will live a half-life. I peek over at Lucas, who isn't even looking at the menu but checking something on his phone. It amazes me how unbothered he can be at times.

Lucas and I met through a mutual friend, and the connection between us had been instant. We speak non-stop, and he's always a text away when he's not with me. We restaurant-hop a lot—it's an experiment we are carrying out, and so far, this is our fourth venue.

The waiter returns, and I request for *dun dun pelu ata din-din*, with a bottle of water. Lucas orders the same, and I shake my head at him. How original. We're meant to be experimenting and trying out different foods. He just shrugs at me and goes back to his phone. After waiting for him to acknowledge my presence, I finally break and say something.

"So, Lu. Are we going to talk, or are you going to be glued to your phone?"

There is guilt on his face as he smiles sheepishly at me before reluctantly putting his phone away. Reluctantly because he paused to think before deciding keeping it aside was the best option. He is looking at me now, his facial expression asking me *now what*.

I roll my eyes at him. This is bad. There has never been an awkward moment between us. Come to think of it, I'm usually the one talking non-stop. I don't get why most guys I tend to fall for don't like talking and let me ramble away for there not to be a lag in the conversation.

"Sewa, I believe I know you fairly well by now, so whatever is it that's eating you right now, I'm all ears."

Am I that noticeably nervous? What did I do to give myself away? And what should I say? What is wrong with me? Lucas is looking at me expectantly, waiting for my reply, and I am at a loss for words.

Luckily for me, the waiter appears, pushing a trolley with our order, and I remember how hungry I am.

I use the excuse of food not to speak or interact with Lucas. I don't think I've ever been this interested in the dishes we have eaten at restaurants before. I'm just glad he lets me be for now.

"What do you think about this restaurant?" I ask once we are done eating and have paid our bills respectively.

The food was excellent, and I especially liked the *ata din-din*, the pepper sauce nicely complementing the fried yam and the small pieces of meat. I would order more, but I don't have the time to wait.

"It's okay, I guess. When are we going to stop restaurant-hopping? I think four is enough."

And there goes my excuse to have us meeting up more than once in a week.

"If you're tired already, then this will be our last. Geez, Lu, you're no fun."

He childishly sticks his tongue out at me, and I shake my head at him. I should do it now, just blurt it out and wait for his reaction. If this was via text, I would send it and turn my phone and everything that allows for a two-way means of communication off.

"Sewa, I think we should get going now. I'll drop you off at home."

"I have something to say to you."

Here I go. I sound so scared—what is wrong with my voice? Lucas looks at me with questioning eyes and smiles. Maybe he's trying to calm my nerves.

"I like you. In fact, I more than like you and want you to be my boyfriend. I don't know about you, but the few weeks I've spent with you have me so in my feelings, and there is nothing more I want."

My heart is beating so fast, my face must be flushed, and I can feel myself slightly shaking as I dare to look at Lucas' face because he still hasn't said anything and is leaving me hanging.

He looks conflicted, and I immediately know our relationship is about to be hit by a BRT bus.

"I'm sorry, Sewa. I agreed to work things out with Chika yesterday. If I had known—"

"It's fine. I understand. No need to justify your answer."

I cut him off before he can go on with his excuses. I'm sad, but it doesn't come like the overwhelming sadness as I had expected. I feel like I'm going to be okay again. I am suddenly very calm.

It's like cold water poured on me and numbed all my feelings.

I look at Lucas and smile. He doesn't smile back and is still looking at me with an expression that pretty much screams pity. It's either we get past this bump in our relationship, or it ends entirely.

"Seriously, Lucas. It's fine. I'll nurse my broken feelings, and I'll be fine. Don't worry, nothing has to change. We can still be friends, right?" I ask him, trying to set his mind at ease.

I don't know why I'm trying to appease him. I'm the one who got rejected.

He nods and motions for us to get up and leave. Since he's my ride, I have no choice but to follow him. When I'm home, I'll have time to regroup and process what the hell just happened.

CHAPTER TWO

The ride home with Lucas is uncomfortable—I have been working so hard to avoid an awkward lull between us, and now it's hitting us at full mass and I can't help but harbour a bit of bitterness. To make matters worse, we are stuck in typical Lagos mainland traffic. I don't know what on Earth causes the traffic these days, because you can go for hours and not see what would have caused it in the first place.

After more than an hour of uncomfortable silence on a trip that wouldn't have taken more than thirty minutes without traffic, I can't help but be relieved once we get in front of my apartment building. He tries to start a conversation with me about the giant storm cloud hanging over our heads, but I cut him short, making it clear it isn't something I want to acknowledge, at least not anytime soon.

I dejectedly walk into the compound of my home, not having it in me to muster up a smile or say greetings to the gateman and the people with him. Sulking and self-pitying are the only things I can do for the rest of this gloomy day because I know once I sleep on it, I will be fine. I just have to be.

I use my own key to unlock the door and enter the apartment, and I'm in the process of relocking it when I hear my mum cry out in excitement. She is easily excitable; the littlest things can make her so happy. But again, it could be a displeased outcry—she is as easily displeased as she can easily be happy. I hear some sort of ruckus when opening the door leading into the parlour from the entryway of the apartment, to then be greeted by the sight of my mum and her boyfriend, Mr. Saludeen, embracing and kissing like they don't have a care in the world.

Oh my goodness! How many times do I have to walk in on them making out? I clear my throat loudly, and the happy couple untangles from each other, like high school teenagers that have been caught red-handed in a compromising position together. My mum turns a bright shade of red while Mr. Saludeen smirks at me, looking very pleased with himself. My mum peers at me sheepishly, but I know she's happy; she is practically glowing. I'm glad she seems to have found herself a good man to love and who loves her back. I see it in the way he watches her and is always there without her needing to ask.

"Adesewa, you're back home early today. Any problem?"

"I'm fine, Mum. Aren't I allowed home again? I didn't know you had plans to be home, either."

Mr. Saludeen only chuckles and sits down on a sofa. My mum also sits, and he tucks her at his side. What is going on? Why are they more than affectionate in front of me? Are they somehow trying to mock me that they are in a happy relationship whereas I am not?

Okay, I am overreacting.

"How was your day? Your mother and I are having a pleasure-filled day."

"Oh, really? What did you both do?" I ask before thinking.

Did I really want to know how my mum and her boyfriend spent their *pleasure-filled day*? I reluctantly take a seat on a couch beside them, settling down for the conversation I had initiated and was now going to embark on.

"Yes, we did. We went out to eat, a bit of shopping, we came back here to relax, and now, we are engaged. Your mum said yes."

Wait—what? They are engaged. Wow. Oh, my. I can't believe this. I have joked to my mum countless times, telling her she is still young and should get married again—but now, it is really happening? I completely understand the reason for her excited shriek when I entered the apartment. I most likely arrived right after she said yes and had ruined their happy moment a tiny bit.

Oh, well, but my mum is engaged! I don't think any word can explain or define the kind of glee and joy this news brings up in me. There's no one I know who deserves a happily ever after more than her.

"Oh my God! That's wonderful. I'm so happy for you, Mum! I feel like crying tears of joy. Congratulations to you both! So Mr. Saludeen, what made you decide to pop the question now?"

"It's about time, won't you agree? I love Joké too much, the only option left is to make her my iyawo."

My mum blushes at her fiancé's profession of love and how he'd wished to make her his wife, and I want to puke because they are too cute for me to handle at this moment. I get up and hug the happy couple, knowing they would love to be alone but won't send me away.

I go to my room, and once I am alone, I remember the disaster that was my lunch with Lucas and let out a groan. Falling on my ass was clearly a sign from God.

I dig my phone out of my bag and lie down on my bed. Before my mum comes to disturb me and ask me to write her an engagement announcement message for her to put up on her social media platforms, I decide to get a head start on it. Something simple like "I'm engaged to my love Mr. Saludeen" won't work for my mum. She would want to include a prayer and a gooey message of affection towards him, I'm so sure about that. I also know she would only allow the short and simple one as her WhatsApp status message.

I'm meant to also be celebrating a new development in my love life, I can't help sadly muse. I'll soon be twenty-three, and I'm tired of being single; I'm ready for a meaningful relationship. The last serious relationship I was in ended more than a year ago, time during which I fully embraced being single, loving myself, and just enjoying life.

I feel like I am destined to be alone. Okay, maybe I'm not, but like I won't be able to find my soulmate and everlasting love. I find myself doubting time to time if love indeed exists or it could be the Cupid's arrows with my name on them have been exhausted.

I'm lost in thought when the ringtone I set for my best friend intercepts my mind. She is either worried I haven't updated her about the turnabout of today's event or just wants the details and isn't concerned. I accept the call and put it on speaker.

"Sewa. I have been waiting for you to reply me. You can't just leave me hanging in suspense like that. Don't you fear God?"

"*Haba*, Nafisa, you know it isn't like that. My day just took a weird turn, and I haven't had the time to talk to you. You're not serious. What does fearing God have to do with this? You're such a drama queen."

"Let me guess, that idiot didn't want a relationship with you?"

"You know it. He said he just agreed to work things out with his ex. I guess I was a backup plan or a rebound. I don't even understand. He used me to make his ex jealous. I feel like an idiot."

"Lucas is the idiot. I don't understand why men let a woman who is beautiful in and out, intelligent, smart, beautiful and wonderful like you g—"

"Yes, girl, go off, Nafisa! Rain down the compliments!"

"I'm serious, Sewa. You deserve better than him. You know I don't like him even. He is as shallow as that Lucas on BKChat London."

I love Nafisa so much, she never ceases to amaze me, and I can't help but laugh at the comparison she just made.

"Don't kill me, o. I have heard you. I'll be fine. Thank God I did it now and didn't wait 'til I had invested even more feelings into our relationship. 'Coz I see it now, he would have been with his ex and still playing me like a banjo at the same time."

"You obviously would be fine. In fact, knowing you, you would have gotten tired of him eventually. You can't seem to keep the interest in someone for long romantically. Mrs. Self-Sabotage."

"Shut up, jare! You are meant to be making me feel better." I added the *jare* for emphasis, and the effect is instant.

"*Pele, ma binu.*"

Nafisa rarely apologises so I take it as a win.

"Apology accepted, and I'm not angry. You like to add pepper to everything. You won't believe what just happened!"

"Just tell me, leave the suspense for someone else jo."

"My mum and Mr. Saludeen got engaged. I think I came home when she said yes, 'coz I walked in on them smooching."

"Ah! That is wonderful news! I love this, the wedding party finna be lit! I'm happy Big Mummy is getting married."

"It's true. I've not even thought about the party segments. You're going as far as I am concerned to the wedding party. I know they are also going to have an engagement party. Now at the parties, all my nosey aunts and Mummy's friends will start asking me where my boyfriend is and when my wedding is occurring."

"Who knows if you would have found a boyfriend by that time? Stop acting like you being alone is set in stone. Anything can happen and you know it. Be positive jo."

"It is because you have snagged yourself the perfect man and you're engaged that you're talking like this. Look free me. I'm allowed to be negative for the rest of today if I want to. You can call me out on my sulkiness from tomorrow, but today, allow my moping. But forget me jo, how are you?"

"I'm great. My life is as perfect as it can be, and I couldn't be more thankful. Nothing new is going on in my life. If not, you will be the first to know. Anyway, before I forget, are you ready for your interview tomorrow?"

"I'll be fine. I don't think anyone can ever be ready for an interview. I just have to be calm and collected, and I believe I'll ace it. I've got all the right qualifications for it."

"That's the spirit. The other people who didn't want you don't know what they have lost. Okay, Sewa baby, I've got to go. My mum needs me for something, I wonder how she will survive without me when I move into my husband's house. Talk later, love you!"

"Love you, too."

I manage to squeeze my reply before the call ends.

I come up with many announcement posts to show my mum, with the assistance of Nafisa, so she will have a variety to choose from, but she still complains when I present them to her and makes me come up with a new one with her input.

I take an Instagram-worthy picture of her hand, showcasing the engagement ring, and use the platform to share the image and message, so it will also post on her Facebook wall, killing two birds with one stone. I argue that she need not put the same words for her WhatsApp status, and when Mr. Saludeen agrees with me, she lets me set it as the short and simple message, along with changing her profile picture to one of her and him.

Pleased I have that out of the way, I go into the kitchen to see what I can have for dinner. I don't feel like eating what is being made for dinner, semolina and èfó riro, that Yoruba dish prepared with vegetables and stock fish, palm oil, crayfish, pepper, locust bean and also sometimes meat and other ingredients. I decide to eat boiled plantains with the èfó riro, not a fan of the semo, disliking the coarse durum wheat rubble used to make pasta and couscous usually.

After a pleasant and filling meal, I go back to my room to get ready for bed, which involves taking a bath, my facial care routine, and brushing my teeth. I have to brush them religiously if I don't want to lose any more of my molars.

I contemplate messaging Lucas, but seeing that he had not bothered to text or call me, I decide against it. Instead, I chat with my friends, browse through all the apps I love using, and check for entertainment while listening to music before I settle on a book I would read 'til sleep found me.

CHAPTER THREE

I don't know how to be fashionably late—the so-called Nigerian way of keeping to time kills me. I was asked to come for an interview by ten a.m. Monday morning, and me being the punctual person that I am got here twenty minutes before. In this office setting, they are still on Nigerian time, where when they give an actual time, it means two hours later.

Palm and Co. is a book publishing firm. I interviewed for the role of designer, where I will be one of the people responsible for the designs being created for the books. I would ensure that the covers and interior designs are in line with the message the manuscript is passing across, finished according to schedule, and error-free. I'll also be working alongside the authors to diligently publish their books.

This firm is relatively new, and in three years, they have successfully published and pushed out twenty-plus books by Nigerian authors, but not just any books— they always find the gems. Their literary scouts are very good; I can even call them the best here. Apart from that, they are moving with times by not focusing solely on traditional book publishing. Their online presence is massive and has a following of thousands across their different online platforms. What caught my attention about this firm is the book designs: they are beautifully done and support the tales the books tell. I was so thrilled when I got called back for an interview.

My interviewers loved my portfolio and my artistic outlook, and it was even a plus that I knew how to make use of drawing and designing applications. I know I'm going to fully adapt to being a member of staff here, because so far so good, every person I came across has been warm and welcoming.

After the unsatisfying job I was given by the government for the duration of my NYSC year, as a secondary school English teacher, I knew a change of scenery would do me good, especially pursuing an occupation I have a passion for, with people I can relate with.

I know my brother, Demola, will be very happy with our mum and Mr. Saludeen getting engaged. Mr. Saludeen is the only dad figure he has ever honestly had, and Demola looks up to him. This year marks the tenth anniversary of our dad's death, and it's undoubtedly past the time our beautiful mum gets hitched again—she isn't even near fifty yet. As for me, I hope he does not expect me to call him dad or daddy because it would just be awkward and wrong. I might call him Baba—it's more ominous and nationally accepted as a respectful term to call our male elders. I think sticking to Mr. S will do just fine.

"Sewa, look out!"

But the warning is too late, and I walk into a glass wall, hitting my head hard and bouncing away from the door. I immediately clutch my forehead due to the resounding pain, and my breathing becomes harsh as I let out pathetic whimpers. Someone softly draws me 'til I'm sitting down, and the person's hand starts rubbing my back soothingly.

"We need to stop meeting this way."

I know that voice. Now I want to die of embarrassment. How is it possible that the same stranger who managed to knock me on my ass also gets to watch me daydream myself into a glass wall? It always amuses me what my mind can manage to be stressing over when I am feeling physical pain. I peek at him, and his beautiful face is wearing a look of amusement tinged with worry. Once he notices me glancing, the worry on his face eases, and he smiles at me.

I drop the hand that was hiding my face and look around. The receptionist smiles and says sorry to me, and I'm glad only she witnessed the latest episode of me being a klutz. My head throbs just a little, and my forehead is a bit tender when I feel it, but hopefully, I won't get a bump.

"You remember my name." I roll my eyes at myself for saying such a dumb thing. Of course he does. He freaking just called it out. I need to redeem myself. "I mean, you do, obviously. I just wasn't expecting it. You're right, we should stop meeting like this. My body can only take so much."

His smile widens, and I know I need to stop talking with my foot in my mouth.

"I'm Jide. Jide Harriman. How is your forehead?"

"It will live. It's nice to make your acquaintance, Jide Harriman, finally."

"Do you work here?"

"I hope to. What about you?"

"Something like that. I am the latest investor in this firm."

"So if I do get the job, you're going to be technically my boss?"

"Technically."

He says the technically with a smirk, and it makes me laugh. That's when I sight the time and the curious glances the receptionist keeps throwing at us. I've not even gotten a job here, but I know she's going to be on my case about Jide when she sees me next.

"I best be on my way. I've spent more time than I planned here already. It was nice meeting you again, despite the circumstances," I say with a small laugh and get up.

He gets up with me; I guess he is also leaving. He makes a show of opening the glass door for me, and I roll my eyes at him then turn around to wave goodbye to the receptionist.

"Do you have anything pressing to do now?"

My heartbeat tripled. Do I say yes or no? I know I'm somewhat attracted to him, but answering yes will make me seem easy. But if I say no, I'll leave it to chance to bump into him again. I ignore my mind telling me to say yes and play hard to get.

"Why do you ask?"

"I'm not ready to part with your company is all. I have enjoyed our interactions."

He looks at me when he says that, and my face heats up and I know he knows what his words are doing to me because his smile grows bigger.

"Let's go for lunch? There we can introduce ourselves formally, and I'll make sure you don't hurt any part of your body when you're with me."

"You will never let my embarrassing moments go, will you? I don't have anything pressing to get to. I usually free up my day whenever I have a job interview, due to being a victim of Nigerian time one to many times."

"I can't ever. No one can beat our first encounter story. It's that epic."

"Enjoy yourself."

"Did you drive here?"

"Nope, I don't have a car. At least, not yet."

He smiles down at me, and my stomach immediately fills up with butterflies. Something is seriously wrong with my hormones these days, the way I'm crushing and liking men left to right. It's not my fault, though. Lucas has made our relationship estranged, and I seem like a stalker, all in the name of keeping our friendship.

My guy is ignoring my texts, and the messages aren't dangerous or anything. I'm like '*Hi, how's your day?*' and he'll reply me two hours later, with some minor words and then ignore me until the next day. Someone who used to reply my texts to him immediately. It baffles me how he is acting as if I rejected him when he is the one who put me in the friend zone. I'm done trying with him—I wish him and Chika all the best. I'm still a bit butt-hurt, but I'm a big girl and I know I'll be fine, I think sooner than later.

Jide leads me to his fancy-looking car. He opens the passenger side door for me, which surprises me, how many Nigerian men take the time. He might just as well be acting chivalrous to impress me. If that's the case, well, colour me impressed.

I'm buckling my seatbelt as Jide opens the door to the driver's seat and gets in. He hands me his AUX cord, and I eye him. Is he trying to judge my taste in music? Why is he just assuming I like music?

"Is there anyone you would like to tell you're with me? So your mind will be at ease, in case I turn out to be your worst nightmare, they'll know who to look for?"

I turn to look at him sharply. He is right, for the thought has crossed my mind, and I was secretly going to text Nafisa, but since he brought it up …

"Hand me your phone, please."

He unlocks it and gives it to me. I dial my number on it, to get his number, not for him to dictate it to me. I hand him back his phone, and he proceeds to store my number. I then quickly send a text off to Nafisa, stating his name, phone number, and how he's an investor in *Palm and Co.* if they need to start searching for me. I also promised to call her later and explain myself in detail when I get home.

I store his name on my phone and go to Snapchat and remove my Snapchat Bitmoji location from ghost mode, so my friends and family on it can see my current spot and track my movements.

"Now that your security is out of the way, it's time for mine."

I laugh; he has to be joking. How would I hurt him? I didn't initiate this, and I have no hidden agenda. Not saying he has, but I'm only going with his flow.

"Come on, Sewa. Don't be a double standard."

He can't be serious. I look at him, and his face is sombre, then he breaks into a smile and lets out a chuckle. This man likes pulling my leg.

"I'm joking. Besides, you gave me your number without me asking, I must point out proudly, and I've texted it to my guy like I assume you just did to a friend or sibling. Just to be safe."

He winks at me, and I just shake my head at him. We both smile at each other before he turns his attention to the road as he starts driving.

"Where are we going for lunch?"

"I know a place."

"Where is this place at, Mister just to be safe?"

"Sheraton."

"Why are we going to Sheraton, the hotel?"

"Yes, the hotel. We are going to a restaurant there, Crockpot."

A restaurant I haven't been to or heard about, but apparently, is going to be fancy, because of my few trips to Sheraton. Sheraton is a popular place where rich people go to carry out trysts, and where I've always encountered many Oyinbos. It's like it's a home away from home for them white folks on the mainland.

"Is the food any good?"

"You'll just have to wait and find out yourself, don't take my word for it. Won't you play music?"

"Why did you just assume I would play music?"

"'Coz it's the polite thing to do? If you haven't noticed, I'm trying to impress you, so you will agree to see me again."

"Don't get so ahead of yourself. We haven't even gotten to the restaurant. Fine. I'll be the DJ, but don't pass any negative comment about my taste in music."

"No backchat from me, ma'am."

There is no way he won't like the songs I play. If he doesn't, then something is wrong with his ears when it comes to sound vibing tunes.

I open my music app and search for Lady Donli and hit shuffle for all her songs. Good for me the first song that plays is 'Cash.'

CHAPTER FOUR

"So, how old are you?" I cut to the chase, really curious about his age.

For one, he looks like he is in his early thirties—he carries himself with a self-assured, confident gait, and his mere presence is arresting. It is all so alluring, and he must be doing more than fine in his choice of occupation if he can invest in organisations such as *Palm and Co.*

"I'm twenty-eight, and you?"

I think my eyebrows shoot up because he gives me a funny look. Before I can reply with my age, he asks me why I am looking at him in a funny way.

"I expected you to be in your thirties. I'm twenty-two."

We have arrived at the hotel, and he shakes his head at me as he finds a parking spot and turns off the car. I immediately open the door and get down, patiently waiting for him to lock the vehicle and lead the way to the restaurant from the car park. Once he's out, he moves to walk beside me, and his hand falls to the small of my back, gently leading me. I hope he can't feel the way my heartbeat increased because of his little gesture.

People smile politely at us, and it's not just me who can feel the aura of importance he exudes because the whole staff is eager to please and accommodate us.

We are seated opposite each other at the back of the restaurant in a quiet corner for two. Our assigned waitress hands out a menu to both of us before leaving, to give us time to decide on what we want to eat.

I was too excited to eat this morning due to the interview, so I decide to order something brunchy and within my price range. I opt for three-egg omelette minus the mushrooms, with a side of potatoes and chicken sausages.

"I'll have the same, and two bottles of water. Thank you," Jide says politely to the waitress after I order my food.

When she leaves, he rubs his hands together and smirks at me. Oh, boy, I wonder what he's about to say.

"I have a bazillion questions to ask you. For example, what job are you applying for at *Palm and Co.*? What is your middle name? Your hobbies? When is your birthday? And most importantly, are you single?"

That is a lot of questions for me to answer. Why does he want to know my middle name? That's just random.

"Would it matter if I am in a relationship?"

"Yes. Because I'll have to respect your relationship with your significant other and only pursue a friendship with you. Answer my questions with an actual answer this time around. Don't worry, I'll also be forthcoming with mine."

"I'm not in a relationship. In fact, I got rejected recen—"

"Noo!" Jide exclaims so dramatically, I can't help but let out a little laugh and nod in agreement.

I know, right? Why would someone reject wonderful me?

"Yes, yes. By the guy who came to meet me at that restaurant. I swear that place cursed me that day."

"I don't believe so. Look where we are now. It somehow led us into each other's lives, and I know that is a good thing."

"You are right about that, Jide. So, what about you?"

"What about me?"

"Are you single?"

"What do you take me for? Of course I am, and I've never been gladder."

"Why are you offended? You asked me, and I wasn't offended. Besides, friends or acquaintances go for outings platonically, and it is what we are doing, after all."

"I thought this was a date." He winks at me before he continues, and no, the wink was not a tacky one; it was quite hot. "I apologise. I had to ask. After all, I've seen you with a man prior to today, and it would do no good to just assume."

I wave him off, not really needing his apology when I know no harm had been intended, and it was a sort of easy banter.

"My middle name is Dolce, my birthday is on the tenth of August. I want to be a creative editor. I like designing covers, fonts, and the likes. Designing is a huge passion of mine, and *Palm and Co.* is a savvy with times Nigerian publishing firm. I can't wait to be a member of the team. I love eating, especially trying out new places and foods. I love reading novels. No, not erotica. Well, not strictly erotica. I also enjoy reading fantasy, mystery, romance novels, and much more. I can go on and on. I love listening and discovering wonderful sounds. Music is a huge part of me, and finally, I love exploring my creative side. I dabble with creative endeavours, I create whenever I am inspired—things like greeting cards, book designs, poems, art, whatever floats my boat at that moment."

Jide listens to me attentively, not once interrupting me, and I like that. I'm glad that he seems genuinely interested in what I have to say.

"I love how you go after what you want. It's refreshing hearing people talk about things that make them happy. And you're going for a job you have a passion for, that is amazing."

"Thank you on behalf of everyone who talks about things they love with passion."

The waitress returns and apologises for the delay, saying the potatoes are almost ready and our food would be with us shortly, and to show how sorry they are for the delay, they give us a mini-plate of shrimp and mayonnaise spring rolls, my favourite.

When she leaves again, and I help myself to a spring roll, Jide seizes the table and starts talking about himself.

"I am a software engineer, a programmer. I design websites, create applications, and many other things that involve the writing of code. I am very good at it, if I must say myself. When I was your age, I created an application, which—I didn't know then—would change my life forever. You probably know it. Druin, the online card games empi—"

"No way! You created Druin. I can't believe it! I'm addicted to it. This is so amazing. I'm so glad I know the owner now. I have so many complaints."

He laughs and shakes his head at me, but I am being very serious. I do love the game; playing Druin is my favourite past-time. I play against many other users worldwide, and the beauty of it is that it is mostly a free app, no in-game advertisements that lead you to pesky sites, just the usual buy-game currency or whatever so you can play immediately instead of waiting for your turns to refill themselves and other deals to buy.

But I've gotten ripped off by the game—once, my account got unceremoniously deleted, and I had to start from the beginning again due to major changes to the application, and the bots that play against us humans cheat. As they are unfair, and luck is very rare in the game, it takes many tries to successfully win a hand.

He stops laughing when he sees my serious face and proceeds to hear me vent about his game. He listens to me attentively, all the while wearing a dismissive smirk.

"I sincerely apologise about that. There were a few hiccups during the upgrade, but I'm glad you still stuck around, and I'm impressed. You have been playing it for a long time, one of the early fans, I see. I hope the game is up to par now, though, no more account troubles, I believe, and your only complaint from what I can tell is that you suck at Druin."

Can you imagine? I roll my eyes at him, and he chuckles. I'm about to go at him when I see the waitress arriving with our food, and I let it go for now. She sets the plates before us, and I want to drool at the sight and smell before me: the food looks and smells so appealing.

"Bon appétit," I say before focusing on the offering before me.

I love Irish potatoes, and these are done so wonderfully well, my taste buds are salivating. When I eat, my full focus is on the food, so I can savour it well. I rarely speak when I'm eating good food, which is one of the reasons why I've been dubbed Foodie by many of my friends.

Halfway through my meal and I randomly glance at Jide to see that he is watching me eat. I start to think of how I have been eating, hoping I've not embarrassed myself too much if he has been watching me for a long time.

"You're not enjoying your meal?"

"I am, but it is appealing watching you eat and the little sounds of delight you make when the taste is favourable to you."

I feel the blood rushing to my face and know he can see me blush, darn light skin problems. I can't believe I am making sounds—well, sounds that are loud enough for him to hear. Sometimes, I just can't help myself.

I shrug at him, sticking my tongue out at him like a child before going back to my meal. I make sure I don't make any more sounds or look at him until I finish my food, which is when I proceed to pour water into a glass cup and drink. I clean my mouth and my hands before dropping the napkin I had placed on my lap back on the table.

"That was one hell of a good meal. I'm going to come back here to have it one of these days when I'm craving something good," I say to Jide, who is now drinking a cup of water.

Once he is done, he nods at me, and the waitress appears with the bill. She goes to hand it to Jide, and I want to roll my eyes, but I hold it back and ask her, "What if I am the one paying?"

She smiles and looks at me apologetically before she hurriedly clears the table of our plates and leaves us alone. When she goes, Jide is looking at me quizzically, and I give him the same look, I think.

"You're something else, Sewa. I invited you to lunch, so I am going to pay."

"I can pay for my meal. Also, it's not going to break my bank or anything. When my friends and I go out, we pay for our meals individually. I'm used to it," I say by way of explanation, which is the truth. I'm trying to break the tradition of relying heavily on men, one I used to follow. It makes me feel very independent to do so.

"Well, this is a date since you didn't object when I named it a date earlier, and I'm paying, so please let it go."

"Fine. I'll treat you next time."

The smile that lights up his whole face as soon I said that almost leaves me breathless. Please, God, don't let me be in over my head and let me ruin this before it even starts.

"If that's what you want, and I'm glad you also want us to have a next time."

Who wouldn't? He is fabulous company, and I'm surprisingly comfortable around him; he is just so easy to interact with. I smile at his response, glad I might not be alone in the infatuation department when it comes to us.

CHAPTER FIVE

I got sent an email before being called by the head of Human Resources at *Palm and Co.* four days after the interview, informing me that I officially had the job if I still wanted it, and I would start work the next Monday. Since then, I've been all about sorting my wardrobe and putting clothes together for work.

The email I had contained an introduction pdf file, telling me the rules and regulations of the firm and its staff, such as how to dress, what time I should be at work, what to do and not do in order not to get fired, etc. Mum and I were ecstatic about me getting my first job all by myself, and that night, both of us went out for a celebratory dinner at our favourite Chinese restaurant, Zen Garden at Ikeja GRA.

While there, aside from talking about me and how she hopes I exceed beyond their expectations and climb my way to the top, she was equally excited to talk about her upcoming wedding and the changes her marriage would bring.

Mr. Saludeen has a child, a son with a woman he was once with, but never got to marry due to irreconcilable differences—at least, that is what my mum told me. The woman left the country and is now happily married with a family of her own. Tosin, Mr. Saludeen's son, is four years older than me, twenty-six. I've seen him only a couple of times over the course of his dad and my mum's relationship. He doesn't stay in Nigeria much, just when he has holidays—he comes to visit his dad, or a friend of his invited him to a wedding, etc. His and his mum's lives are in Canada.

We are friends to an extent—we talk every other day and keep updated with the happenings in our life. We both want our parents to be happy because they deserve to be. Demola admires him. Sometimes, I think he loves Tosin more than he loves me, but I'm not jealous. I'm glad he has a young adult he can talk to and ask advice about manly things.

Mum wants the wedding to be held two months from now. Since she already had a big wedding and she isn't young anymore, she said there isn't a need for the day to be a big extravagant production, because she's saving that for my and Demola's weddings. She isn't picking *aso-ebi*, a specific fabric design, to sell to the people that will come for the wedding, but going for a colour scheme, and two colours will do just fine.

Because she isn't selling aso-ebi to her friends doesn't mean that she isn't selling to her and Mr. Saludeen's family members. Her two sisters with their husbands, one brother with his wife, along with their children, have an aso-ebi material, as they will be wearing the same cloth material with Mr. Saludeen's only other sibling, his younger brother along with his wife and two children. We the children of the couple—I, Demola, and Tosin— will also have our own aso-ebi to differentiate us from the masses.

My mum's family is enormous—I have many cousins and relations through marriage because of it. Aside from her having a huge family, she also has an army of friends, the amount being endless, and I know in the end, her closest of friends will end up having their own aso-ebi. Not a big production of a wedding, my ass.

She's getting a wedding planner to speed along the process—all she and Mr. Saludeen will have to do is approve the samples and whatnot concerning the wedding that the planner brings forth. I'm so glad because planning a wedding is stressful, and when my mum is stressing, there is never peace.

We are also moving out of our apartment. She and Mr. Saludeen decided to buy a house, one where they can both create new memories in. The apartment lease won't be up until the end of the year, so I pleaded to remain in it until then, and she's agreed for now. After the wedding, they are going on their honeymoon, and they are taking Demola along to wherever it is they decide to go since he would be on his summer break by that time, lucky fellow. I think she only agreed to me remaining in the apartment because she won't want me to be alone in a new place for certain months without them around.

She would also be shopping for furniture on her honeymoon for her new home, which I know I'll grow to love when I eventually move there. My room is the only one on the ground floor. Three bedrooms are on the first floor along with a mini parlour. Demola would take one of the rooms, the remaining for guests or Tosin when he is staying over, and finally, the second floor is a suite for the newly wedded.

All I have heard non-stop since the dinner is wedding talk; there is no peace in the apartment anymore. Every day, different groups of friends or the same one plus another set will arrive, and the ruckus these grown women make will put the young girls who think they are loud and wild to shame.

I can tell Mr. Saludeen is also tired of the constant guests who refuse to leave until it's late. I think everyone including my mother is relieved that Sunday has finally come and we can head peacefully to Demola's school for his speech and prize-giving day doubling as a visiting day also at his secondary boarding school.

We make it there before we can miss any significant occurrence. The family sharing a table with us informs us the program only just started and we thankfully arrived after the national anthem, school anthem, opening prayer, and speech had been said.

I hate prize-giving day. It's long, with speeches by guests, usually prominent in something or who have achieved a lot, called to instil inspiration into the youth to work and do better when it comes to their education. But I also feel like it brings a lot of the other students down, seeing their fellow mates or friends collecting awards, plus all the praise they receive—it tends to make the students who are giving everything they got and not skyrocketing with their results feel lowly about themselves.

I'm not saying the people who excel do not deserve praises or awards—it's a two-way street. My thoughts on this came mainly because I was one of those hardworking students who tried their hardest for their works to be spectacular and could only be a bit above average or average.

I'm just glad my mum knew I tried my hardest and didn't make or let me feel stupid when the time came for her to view my reports. I love my mum. Demola is going to hear all about her and Mr. Saludeen's engagement and all the changes that will be happening, and I can't wait for his reaction.

I can't see the little troublemaker in the sea of uniformed children, and I know when the event is over, he will come and find us. Mum and Mr. Saludeen are busy murmuring to each other beside me, lost in their own world, when a message notification from Jide pops up on my lock screen. Without even knowing what it is that he has said, a smile touches my face. I haven't seen him since Monday, but he leaves me sweet messages throughout the day and calls me at night to talk about the happenings in our lives.

I immediately unlock my phone to read the message.

Jide: Your beauty makes what you have one even more stunning.

I'm confused by his words. How does he know what I am wearing? Unless he is here or he saw me somewhere? I look up from my phone and take a look around.

I don't have to look long because I soon find his eyes watching me from across the room, and my heartbeat dramatically increases when he smiles at me before looking away. He is seated at a table in front of the room, near the stage. What is he doing here?

Then I remember what he said last night—he is a guest speaker today, and the school he was talking about is my brother's school. Because of all his accomplishments at a young age, he is indeed remarkable and an honoured guest speaker. I bet he is and will be a role model for many people and children around Nigeria.

Jide: It's a welcomed surprise seeing you here. Although I had an inkling I would see you here, I prayed and wished for this school to be your brother's school, and it seems I have had my way.

My mood immediately improves now that I have something to look forward to, anticipating his speech. Many times over the course of the program, both I and Jide catch each other's eyes, and each time, we both smile and look away. I'm glad I'm not the only one who can't seem to glance elsewhere for long.

"Sewa, who is that young man you've been smiling at?"

I look at my nosey mum, who apparently has been watching me eyeing Jide from across the room. She is looking at me with a funny expression, but I can see the eagerness for juicy information. I'm not going to satisfy her with an answer, though.

"He's someone I know."

She wants to fish for more but stops when they announce Jide's name and he gets up to rounds of applause. Her eyebrows go up when she hears his accomplishment in his short but excellent introduction.

He takes the stage, his face bright with his smile and oozing sexiness to the crowd. With his magnanimous aura, he proceeds to wow both the children and parents with his speech. I know he wowed the children because all of them were paying close attention to what he had to say. He has a natural flow, and his speech is far from boring—it is entertaining, he knows his audience, so he knows what will capture their attention.

Like I assumed, Demola immediately comes to us once the program ends, and he happily hugs me before doing the same to my mum and slightly prostrating to Mr. Saludeen. I take a full look at my younger brother, and I'm alarmed by what I see.

He has lost so much weight. His baby fat has melted. Oh, secondary school is so hard, especially in the first year. This is his first time away from home. He was a day student rather than a boarder for the first and second term. When the third arrived, he wanted to be a boarder. He claimed he was missing out on a lot of activities his friends took part in after school and was tired of feeling left out.

This is his first visiting day I am present for since I wasn't around for his earlier one, back at the end of May. Now, it is the end of June, and the school has its visiting day every last Sunday of a month.

"Chai! You no dey eat abi?" Pidgin leaves my mouth before I can catch myself; I dislike the fact he isn't eating right. Seriously? Nigerian Pidgin to punctuate such a phrase?

He dares to roll his eyes at me.

"The food is terrible, Sewa. I miss yours or Mum's food."

"Hmm baby of the house. It's the life you chose, deal with it. How's school been?"

"It's okay. Everything is great aside from the food."

"Okay, I'm glad to hear that, and I'm sure the food isn't even that bad. You're just a baby."

"I'm not a baby anymore, Sewa. Mum, am I still a baby?"

"Omo kekere ni e, o le da toju ara e. Kilode ti o jeun?"

I laugh at how that backfired. Mum is glaring at him now. He will always be her baby, and she hates when we don't eat and take care of ourselves. I know the next thing she's going to spew about is how Demola is going to make himself sick and give himself an ulcer. And I was right. In the next heartbeat, she goes off about sickness and stomach ulcers.

"Mummy nau," he cajoled. "I just miss your food, and I take care of myself. I make sure I eat at least once a day."

Mr. Saludeen just watches our exchange with a smile on his face, and our mum ignores Demola's protest.

"Demola, as a growing boy, you know you're meant to eat more food. If the food is a problem, I will drop a complaint with the school authorities and get to the bottom of this bad food."

Demola smiles widely at what Mr. Saludeen says, and I just roll my eyes. Of course, he will listen to what Mr. Saludeen says.

"Guess what, your mum and Mr. Saludeen are engaged!"

Demola's eyes almost pop out of his sockets, and I want to laugh. He looks from Mum to Mr. Saludeen, and both of them have huge grins on their faces and are now holding hands as they nod yes to the unspoken question in his eyes.

"No way. I can't believe this. Finally!"

We all start laughing, and Demola gets up to hug Mum and Mr. Saludeen before he excitedly starts asking them questions about the marriage and what it would mean. As I expected, he takes the news very well. He will quickly adapt to the changes.

We are sharing pizza, chicken, and drinking while talking about the happenings in our lives when we are interrupted by no other than Jide Harriman himself.

This man is so forward. With only one supposed date, he is already jumping to meet my parents. I widen my eyes at him, and he winks at me before he speaks.

"Good afternoon, ma'am and sir. I am Jide Harriman, and it's a pleasure to meet you. And you, young man, must be Demola?"

Demola nods eagerly. Mr. Saludeen smiles and exchanges a greeting also. My mum, on the other hand, is looking at both of us curiously. I roll my eyes at Jide and speak up.

"Jide is a friend of mine. He is my boss sef, the job I recently got, he is an investor. As you heard, he is a self-made millionaire whose net worth is increasing daily. Jide, as you know, Demola is my brother, the beautiful woman before you is my mother, Joké Adedotun. Mr. Tolu Saludeen, the man beside her, is her fiancé and our soon-to-be stepfather."

I know I surprised Jide, but he hides it well. Instead, he starts a minor conversation with my mum and Mr.

Saludeen, congratulating them on their engagement, and my mum being the nosey person she is starts asking him personal questions about his life. So I need to come to his rescue and stop my mum's hungry claws from sinking into him and getting matchmaking ideas into her head.

"Jide, please, can you walk with me? I need to talk to you about something."

With that, I drag him away from my mum's presence. He places his hand on the small of my back, and I want to swoon all over again as we leave the table behind. Once we are far enough, he starts chuckling.

"Isn't it too soon to meet the parents?"

"If you're down, I'll introduce you to my family as soon as today," he teasingly says.

I just shake my head at him. We stop in front of a building that doesn't have any traffic made up of people who are moving around.

"Can this be our second date?"

"What?"

"We just attended an event together."

"Jide, you're funny o. Together ke? We came separately with different agendas. You're not serious sef."

"You look beautiful. The image of you in my memory doesn't do you justice. I need to see you more often, not by chance meetings."

"Okay."

My voice sounds so low and shy, and I can't help but blush at his compliments. I'm thrilled he has finally brought up us meeting up again. After Lucas, I'm taking a break from being so forward.

I don't see it coming immediately, so I am caught by surprise when his lips lightly press up against mine. An electrifying jolt goes through my body, and it isn't like the kiss was up to ten seconds.

"I've wanted to kiss your alluring lips, and they are as soft as I've imagined them to be."

I look around to see if anyone noticed what occurred, but no one is paying us any attention. Jide's hands take mine, and he smiles down at me.

"My mum could have been watching, Jide!"

"So what? It's not like you're a little girl anymore, and I just want everyone to know you're mine, and all the other men that have been looking at you to know to back off."

"Jide, you should know I'm not interested in them."

CHAPTER SIX

I've never been as glad for the weekend as I am today. Don't get me wrong—I'm happy with my new job, and it has been a great week adjusting to my new workspace, which is incredible. Everyone is friendly, accommodating, and helpful to the point where I feel at home and envision myself growing and enhancing my knowledge and skills when it comes to creative work.

The creative department is on the third floor. Each unit has its level. The team consists of five long-term staff as the firm can hire freelance photographers and designers if the need arises. There is the head of department, Mrs. Bethany Anobi, who oversees everything and manages us. Diekolola Amao and I are the on-ground designers, Marka Danjuma is the department finance accountant, and James Adeolu is the department's secretary.

Each of us has our private office—except James because his desk is in the reception area of our floor. Unlucky for me, mine is beside the toilet, but no mishap has happened where I have had to endure the smell of something horrid, at least not yet because everyone except Mrs. Anobi uses this toilet. Of course, the head has to have a personal one.

The other rooms consist of a studio for everyone to work together or for freelancers. A conference room for official meetings, a storage room, and a kitchen—which you can't precisely cook in but it has a water dispenser, microwave, kettle, a wall cupboard stocked with kitchen utensils, a table for four, and a basin for washing the utensils.

I assisted Dieko on two projects he was working on, and when we presented them to the different authors, they fell in love and couldn't decide which of the multiple designs to use. That was all I did this week, apart from adjusting and getting to know the people around the offices. We did not acquire any new publishing rights or author this week, and some of the manuscripts hadn't been cleared yet, so no new brief on what to design or create.

Lucky for me, my work best friend Dieko has a car, and he passes my estate on his way home, hence him dropping me off in front of my estate gate since my first day. I've been looking forward to today since Wednesday because my girlfriends and I had decided to have our monthly girls' night out tonight.

I have three girlfriends. I've known Nafisa ever since secondary school. We instantly became sisters for life within a few months of knowing each other, and ever since then, our relationship has stood strong through the test of time and remained unchanged by it. Her family is my family, and mine is hers.

Onyinyechi became my friend when she transferred to our school at the start of senior secondary school. She is not only adorable but loyal and knows how to make wherever she is lively. Nafisa isn't as trusting as I am when it comes to making new friends, but it didn't take long for her to see what I saw in Onyinyechi and for our friendship to blossom. Onyinyechi went ahead to another continent to attend university, but that didn't stop our friendship from flourishing, and it became something more significant when she returned to the country.

Nnoli became my and Nafisa's friend during our second year at university, under unfortunate circumstances. We went to a private university, with a student body of more than one thousand and five hundred, a relatively small number when compared to the number of students attending other private schools. Because of this, it was quite easy to become popularly known for something amongst the students.

We stumbled upon a distraught Nnoli in front of our hostel on a Sunday evening. We had just returned from Nafisa's house after spending the weekend there. Nnoli was one of the freshers we were friendly with. Nafisa and I mainly stuck to ourselves because we could not relate to many of the students in our school, and we'd soon found out that many of them weren't genuine about the reasons they spoke or interacted with us. It was alarming because people were going about their regular business, coming and leaving; people stood around watching her, but no one was consoling her. The girls she usually went around with were nowhere in sight, and some people were giving her nasty side-eye as they passed.

We approached her and sat with her. I asked her what was wrong, and she proceeded to wail and cry harder. I wasn't comfortable with how people were watching us, and I urged her to please come inside and into our room. It took a lot of pleading but she finally agreed, and when she got into our room, her cries reduced 'til she was silently sobbing.

Nafisa gave her a bottle of water and painkillers to take, and I provided tissues for her to clean her face. Once she was able to control herself and took the pills and drank the water, she thanked us profusely, and when I asked her again what was wrong and how we could be of help, she was surprised we didn't know.

Nnoli nudes leaked that weekend while we were at home, and it instantly became viral. The usual story, of sending naked pictures to boyfriends because they asked or begged for it and instead of protecting those personal images, the receivers are careless with how they keep them. A jealous female, apparently one of her so-called friends, was browsing through the pictures on his phone and saw them. Instead of moving on from it, she sent the images to all his contacts on WhatsApp, and the rest was history.

Her picture was shared all over social media, and people dared to tag her in the posts, many false stories about her promiscuity also shared by people adding salt to the wound. Her boyfriend broke up with her because he didn't want to be with someone everyone had seen naked, and she had allegedly been with too many members of the male sex for his liking. She became labelled a prostitute and was being dragged both online and offline by bullies. People she called her friends turned their backs on her and went ahead to show support to the girl who had leaked the nudes, who claimed it was an accident.

Nnoli had finally reached her emotional breaking point and had just confronted her friends when we'd found her in front of the hostel. We took her under our wing and made sure she understood she wasn't the one at fault and had done nothing wrong except trusting a wicked person or people and even that, she couldn't have known. We made sure that she understood the culture of victim-blaming in Nigeria, especially when it came to girls and women, was wrong and shallow—many people just don't know any wiser and would rather be ignorant and follow the crowd like sheep.

We made sure Nnoli understood that this wasn't the end of her world. That she should always keep her head up, be strong and emulate self-confidence. Even if she didn't feel confident, she should fake it, reminding her that most of the people in our university won't always be in her life nor would they add any value to it and we had her back no matter what, and that's how she became our girlfriend.

Nnoli and Onyinye, as we call her for short, became good friends instantly. In Nnoli's defence, no one can meet Onyinye and not be her friend. Nnoli today is a confident, no-nonsense, and self-assured young woman who no one can mess with or use to their advantage at her disadvantage. She hadn't let that episode in her life cripple her, and she learned a lesson about living from it, albeit a hard one.

Tonight, we are meeting at La Mango at Ikeja GRA to eat, drink, chill, and unwind from our week. It's not like we don't see each other any other day; it's just hard to get us all together in one place, so we use that as an excuse to have a compulsory night out once a month.

While we are there, Nafisa takes every chance she gets to bombard us with her wedding plans, ignoring my constant pleas to take a break from wedding talk because I also have to endure wedding planning talk when I am home from my mummy dearest.

Onyinye is working as the overall head of the social media department for the phone selling organisation Mobile. Mobile has many branches all over Lagos and in several other states, and all the social media managers report to her. Her mother is the owner of Mobile, and one day, Onyinye would head the organisation. Onyinye loves her job, and she takes a lot of pride in how she is growing the organisation's online presence.

Nnoli is doing well, only she is very stressed with her job as an assistant at a government office and wants to find out if she could work elsewhere, but she honestly can't wait to finish her NYSC program so that she can apply for a master's course in marketing.

Onyinye offers to hire her in her department, telling her the work won't be easy but would be fun because she would be in an environment with people near her age and she would also get paid a salary along with her government required fees. Nnoli accepts the offer, and they decide to discuss how it would go on a later day. We instantly see how happy Nnoli becomes and a lot of the stress she was feeling leaving her body. I love how we are there for each other.

After I gush about my working situation to them, Nafisa proceeds to take a break from talking about her wedding to tell them about Lucas, then Jide. I want to kill her for mentioning Lucas, but I preen when they proceed to praise me in the process of bad-mouthing him for turning down an unpriceable wonder like me.

I turn into a blushing fool when it comes to talking about Jide, and I know I won't see the end of being teased by them about how hooked on him I have become in a matter of two weeks. But they all know the beginning is always the sweetest part when you like someone—it's not like I haven't watched them make a fool of themselves when they had desired someone in the past. Even Nafisa still behaves like one when it comes to her fiancé, Sani, and whatever he does for her, even the smallest things that don't need gushing over anymore because she has been dating him for more than two years now.

My phone vibrates. Speaking of the devil, it's a message from Jide. I can't hide the smile that takes over my face whenever his name pops up on my screen, and my girlfriends notice and tease me more about him.

Jide: Sewa love, hope you're having a good time for both of us because I'm still working on this new application and my favourite distraction is too busy for me. I know you said I shouldn't call or text you tonight and you would when you get home, but I couldn't resist I miss you.

I just send him a smiling and heart emoji before putting my phone in my purse. Once done with our foods and drinks, we decide to be a little crazy and have a dance party at our table, entertaining the other people in our vicinity. We take a seat and burst into laughter because Nnoli and Nafisa don't know how to dance, but it never deters them. We buy another round of cocktails and calmly sip on them before we part for the night.

Nafisa and Onyinye offer to drop Nnoli and me off at our respective homes, but I don't want them going out of their ways and driving too late. Besides, Nnoli's home is on the way to Onyinye's place, so her taking Nnoli was more understandable. Sani dropped Nafisa off, and he would be the one to take her home because he didn't trust anyone else to drive his baby late at night.

I don't have a problem with using Taxify. It was what brought me here. I couldn't wait to get home, take a nice warm shower, and talk to Jide a bit to end such a beautiful day.

CHAPTER SEVEN

"Sewa, aso e fine gan. You know ko si big deal ninu style yi ti o ran."

With my back turned so my mum can't see me, I roll my eyes and reply her in my mind. *Yes Mum, I know the fabric is fine, but you're just hating because I didn't sew the style you picked for me and I am also aware there isn't a big deal in the style of my outfit*—a simple short-sleeved gown that flares down from below my breasts to my knees. It's classic, beautiful, and comfortable. One of Jide's friends is getting married, and he asked me to be his date for the event and so he can also introduce me to his friends.

During the week on Tuesday, Jide had come to take me out for a quick lunch during my break at a restaurant near my workplace. My lunch break is one hour, and since I'm still a newbie even if two weeks old, I still have to be the perfect new employee. I made sure we kept to time, and I was returned back to the office before my time was up.

I was very glad he came—I enjoyed being in his company even if I acted like he was a pest. More than a week without seeing him felt more like two months, and that was how I knew I was in over my head for him. It was during this break he told me about the wedding which would be on Saturday and asked me if I would like to accompany him, and my answer was yes.

When he dropped me off back at the office, he removed the bag containing the invitation and aso-ebi from his boot and gave it to me. I laughed because what if I had said no, I would be busy on the day. He said he was being hopeful and that was why he got it already. He offered to pay the amount it would cost to sew the material, but I kindly declined. My tailor and I have our own understanding, and sewing clothes with her are affordable for me.

I am applying nude-coloured lip gloss to my lips to finish my look, peering through my small mirror. I can see my mummy hovering at the entrance of my room, so I know she has something on her mind she wants to address. I don't know why she won't just come out with it already.

"Mummy, what is it?"

She sighs dramatically, enters my room, and lies down on my bed, getting comfortable before she speaks.

"I hope this Jide person is a good man, this one that you won't bring him to the house so I can question him. You can never be too careful these days."

"Haba Mummy, I'll be fine. Nothing can happen, and I have a good feeling about him. Besides, when am I not careful?"

"I'm just saying, Sewa. I hear news every day about young women who get raped, kidnapped, killed, and used for rituals. Many people are not who they pretend to be."

"God forbid o! It will not happen to me, by God's grace. Mum, stop depressing yourself with such thoughts. I am protected, and nothing of such shall befall our family and friends."

"Amen. I've heard you. It's just my reminder for you to be wise and careful. I wish you well in this relationship. I want you to be happy. If this is the man God says is for you, so will it be, and if not, you will still be alright."

"I hear you, and Mummy, I love you."

"I love you, too."

My mum is on her way out of my room when we hear the doorbell go off. She looks at me, and I look at the time. It's five minutes past one, and Jide told me to expect him by one so we can get to the wedding party venue around two or a bit past it, because the wedding is being held on the island and driving from the mainland there will take more than half an hour or more depending on traffic.

"That's him at the door?"

My phone starts ringing, and Jide's name pops up. I nod at my mum, and I know she's going to go and hound him. I quickly select the wedges I'm wearing, spray myself with my perfume, and remove the scarf I had tied to set my edges. I look in my full-length mirror and love what I see staring back at me. I put the invitation, my lip gloss, phone, and wallet into my strapless purse and head for the parlour.

My mum has Jide sitting on the long sofa, a glass cup filled halfway with chilled apple juice along with the carton on a mini-table in front of him. She is on a single couch beside him. She might have been grilling him because Jide is explaining something to her, and she is smiling at him.

He stops speaking once he sees me and stands up, a huge grin is on his face, and the way he is looking at me makes me blush. Take that, Mum. Even if there is no big deal in my outfit, it's clear that Jide thinks I look beautiful in it. His agbada makes him look like someone of importance and so smart—I love how he is wearing his outfit, his fila perched perfectly on his head.

"Sorry, ma, your daughter looks more beautiful each time I see her."

I know my cheeks are out because I can't control the big smile that takes over my face at his compliment. My mum gets up from the sofa and smiles at both of us.

"Let me let you both be going. We'll continue talking another time, Jide. Just be good to my daughter, and she will be good to you also."

"Yes, ma, I will return her to you in one piece. Thank you, ma, for trusting her with me."

I gag. Jide is sucking up to my mum and telling her things she wants to hear, which is extremely cute, but it's making me uncomfortable. I put my hand on his arm and drag him away as I say goodbye to my mum.

Once we are in his car and he starts driving, he goes ahead to talk about how he likes my mum and how cool she is. When I ask him what they had been talking about in the short minutes it took for me to come out of my room, he refuses to answer and just says my mum and him came to an understanding.

The bride is Jide's friend. They went to university together and have kept in touch since then, so I understand now why he said I'm going to be meeting a lot of his friends. I guess a lot of people who went to university with them will be in attendance. I feel a little nervous because I'm going to be at an event where I know only one person, and I know a lot of people's attention is going to be on me, not only as the odd one out but as Jide's date.

The venue is at one of the big event centres on the island. There was little traffic on our way, so we got there a little past two. The place is so full, I'm surprised Jide found space to park his car. He links my arm in his, holding our invitations, and leads me to the entrance. He greets several people but doesn't stop to chit-chat.

The inside of the venue is beautifully arranged, and it's clear that the hall has been divided into two. One part is for the young people, guests of the bride and groom, and the other is for the elders, the guests of the parents. It's also clear that different aso-ebi has been selected for the young and the old.

Jide leads me to the right towards a table with young men and women like him near the stage where the bride and groom comfortably sit. They are all excited to see him, and he receives a couple of hand slaps and greetings from his friends. He introduces me to them as his girlfriend. When he says that, he looks at me like he knows I want to object to his statement, but I will when we are alone.

After that, he leads me to the stage where we congratulate the latest married couple, and he hands the bride an envelope. She hugs him and me, making sure we take a picture with them before releasing us.

Once we are seated, a waiter approaches us and hands us each a menu. I go through the list and decide on eating ofada rice and assorted meat. I give him back the menu, and Jide goes for the same, always copying me.

Jide takes a cup and pours a glass of champagne into it and fills it with ice before he offers it to me, but I kindly decline and ask for a glass of juice instead. I don't want to get slightly intoxicated.

"Finally, I am meeting the lady that has Jide's boxers in a twist. I'm Coker, his best bud."

I didn't notice Coker take the empty seat beside me because I was discussing drinks with Jide, and I smile politely at him. I have equally heard about him on two occasions in passing from Jide who was recounting the crazy things his friend made him participate in.

"And I finally meet the infamous Coker."

He laughs at my response and relaxes into his seat. I turn to look at Jide who smiles and shakes his head at his friend's antics.

"Guy, why are you beside my woman? Go and find your own o," Jide says, and it's my turn to laugh.

Coker is handsome, and clearly, it won't be hard for him to find a woman for himself. In fact, there are plenty of beautiful women sitting at this table for one not to have a thing with him.

The food arrives, and Jide and I instantly dig in. This ofada sauce is killing it, complementing the rice so well. Coker talks to Jide and me as we eat, keeping us good company. I notice a young woman giving me curious looks, her eyes moving from me to Jide and from me to Coker. After catching her trying to stealthy-stare at us for the fifth time, I ask them if they know her, and the groan that leaves Coker's mouth makes me smirk.

I was right in my assumption about one of the women at the table having a thing with Coker. The next time I catch her staring at me, I smile widely at her. She quickly looks away before looking back at me with a you-got-me smile.

Her name is Jumoke. Coker and she were a couple until recently, but since they moved within the same circle of friends, meetings like this will always happen.

Once we're done eating all sort of treats that the waiters and waitresses bring to our table, Jide drags me to the dance floor to bust some moves with the bride and groom, so he can shower them with money as they dance.

Soon, everyone at our table is on the dance floor grooving to the tunes the DJ is playing and having fun. When I get tired, Jide leads us back to our table. We notice it is getting late, and since we are going back to the mainland, we decide it is time for us to go. We say our goodbyes to the married couple and his friends before leaving the wedding venue.

At the car park, once we get to his car, his arm unlinks from mine and goes to hold my waist. He turns me to face him and pulls me in before his lips close over mine, and when I move closer to him, the kiss becomes deeper.

That's how I end up French-kissing someone in an open public space without a care of my surroundings.

CHAPTER EIGHT

"Sewa! I hope you bought what I requested now that you're working."

Demola ambushes me as soon as I step into the apartment as if he has been watching for me. He doesn't even offer to assist with any of the bags I am carrying, only eyeing the white nylons I am holding. He tries to look inside one of the bags, making me hiss as I barge past him into the living room. Let's see if I'll give him anything with that stupid attitude.

Mum is sitting on a sofa with two other women who I instantly recognise as her sisters. Aunties Jumoke and Jola. I immediately drop to my knees and greet them.

"Good evening, Mummy, Aunty Jola, and Aunty Jumoke."

Aunties Jola and Jumoke both have huge smiles on their faces, and they both get up from their seats as they urge me to also stand up so they can each hug me.

"Omo mi, I heard you're working now. You're a big woman now o!" Aunty Jumoke says to me, and I just smile at her and nod—she always starts by calling me the Yoruba word for 'child.' All I want to do is escape to my room so that I can settle down from my very long day.

"When you get your first pay, don't forget us when you're distributing the money! You know it's the tradition," Aunty Jola reminds me.

I nod and watch them take their previous sitting positions beside my mum, using the short lag to escape to my room. I lock the door as soon as I am inside, knowing my brother will just barge in if I don't secure it.

Demola has only been home for one day, and I can't wait for him to go back to school—the boy is so rude. I can't wait for him to go on his summer break with Mum. I don't even feel jealous anymore that he is travelling and I am not. He should just go.

As I am exiting my bathroom, towelling my body dry, my rooms doorknob turns downward. Once the door doesn't budge open, a set of loud rapid raps follow, and I know without a doubt it's Demola. I ignore him and get dressed. His rapid knocking doesn't cease, and my annoyance towards him grows.

I'm going to show him pepper. I look around my room for something that I can hit him with, something that wouldn't do much damage to him but will still sting. I select one of my rubber slippers from my shoe rack. My feet in my in-house slippers, I gently turn the lock on my door, so he doesn't know I'm opening it. I throw the panel open while he is mid-knock, and once he sees what I have in my hand, he starts running, but not before I land a hit on his back. I take off after him.

"Mummy! Sewa is beating me, and I didn't do anything to her!" he screams as he runs, heading for his room. He gets in there and slams the door.

Lucky for me, he doesn't have access to the key to his room, so he can't lock his door. I know he is putting pressure on the panel, but I'm stronger and bigger than him as he is a scrawny little brat. With a mighty push from me, the door opens, and I enter his room. He backs away towards his bed cowering, using his hands to protect his head, and I smirk at my victory.

I hit him two times with my slippers on his back as he pleads for me to please stop, and I'm about to land the third of my intended five hits when our mum and aunts enter the room.

"Sewa, ma pa aburo e o!" Aunty Jola exclaims dramatically when I land my third hit as if I can kill him with a slipper. Demola gets up and sits on his bed, squeezing his face and pretending as if I hit him very hard.

"Kilode, Sewa! Fi aburo e si le," Aunty Jumoke says next, demanding I leave him alone and explain myself. Meanwhile, our mum is looking at two of us like she wants to take the slipper from me and beat us both.

"Mummy, it was Sewa. I was knocking on her door, and she opened it and started beating me."

When he finishes speaking, all eyes turn on me, and the elders are already scolding me with their looks.

"When I came back from work, Demola did not greet me or ask me how my day went. He didn't even offer to carry my bags. Instead, he said *I hope you bought what I requested now that you're working*. No please left his mouth. I was in my room bathing, and when I came out of my bathroom, Demola was trying to break down my door. When he couldn't open it, he started knocking loudly and did not stop for more than five minutes."

I look at Demola and give him the evil eye, but he just smiles at me sheepishly.

"Sewa nau, don't vex for me. How was your day at w—"

"Dake!" Aunty Jola exclaims, telling Demola to shut up before he can finish asking his question. All the elders' scolding eyes are on him now.

"Is that how to apologise to your older sister? Oya, prostrate for her now," Aunty Jola continues admonishing him.

I smirk inside, but my face is expressionless outside, happy that he is getting scolded. Serves him right.

"Leave them alone, that's how they always behave. You would think Sewa would stop stooping to his level and act like the adult she claims she is."

I brace myself to look my mum in the eye after she finishes speaking, and she still appears annoyed with me. She faces Demola, who is sullen and well-scolded, and I know she's about to drop him a scathing comment.

"It's like that your boarding school has erased your home training, abi? Ti mo ba mu e."

Her warning statement, if she gets a hold of him, still hangs heavily in the air as she leaves his room with her sisters in tow. Demola turns to me and frowns. I know how he is feeling—we both hate being scolded by our mum.

"Are you happy now, Sewa?"

"Yes, I am."

"You're such a child."

"As long as my mother is alive, I am always going to be a child to her."

He rolls his eyes at me. I am satisfied, so I head back to my room. He follows me, hot on my heels.

"Sewa, I'm sorry nau, please."

"Abeg jo, you just want me to give you what I bought."

"Please?"

"Whatever. Next time, you'll see if I'll give you anything."

My phone's ringtone is halfway through as I enter the room. I quickly pounce on it and see it's a call from Jide, but as I'm about to click on the green button, it goes off. I promptly give Demola his food so he can leave my room before Jide calls me back.

Instead of a call, my message notification sound comes in, and I pick up my phone to see that I have two missed calls already from him. The message is also from him. I unlock my phone and quickly read his text.

Jide: You've spoilt me so much, I'm shocked you're not answering my calls. Hope all is well and get back to me as soon as possible, need to hear your beautiful voice.

I am about to call him back when my mum is shouting for both me and Demola. I had gotten mixed spaghetti with plantain and chicken for both of us. I carry my food pack with my phone and head to the living room as I text Jide back.

Me: I'm okay, you? I'll tell you when we can talk. Don't miss me too much.

Mum motions for me to take a seat, and as I'm settling down, Demola appears and sits beside me. He thinks he is being subtle with the message he is trying to send to our mum and aunts, that we are no longer fighting. I open my pack of food and start eating.

"Mr. Saludeen and I just finalised on the wedding dates, on the tenth of August is our registry wedding and the next day is for the wedding party. So there's enough time for our honeymoon and still be back in time for Demola to resume school."

I don't know why our mum and aunties give us expectant looks like we have a say in choosing the date or could dare object. Demola shrugs at them and doesn't say anything, but I have questions.

"Mummy, I'm happy for you. Let the rush hour begin since it's two weeks from now. So how big is the wedding reception going to be? Can I invite my friends?"

"Sewa, I've told you it's going to be a small event already. Why are you asking me how big it is going to be? Is it not Nafisa, Nnoli, and Onyinye you're going to invite, and Jide?"

"Yes, but who says Nafisa won't bring Sani, or somebody may follow each of them?"

"It's not a big event, but I'll give you a table for your friends, how is that? The people in attendance will be two hundred tops."

I'm surprised at the number she said. Two hundred guest is small, especially for my mum.

"Mummy, can I go to my room now?" Demola asks and promptly gets released.

I, on the other hand, am bombarded with questions about Jide by my aunties, and my mum proudly boasts about his achievements before the talk returns to wedding planning and deciding the aso-ebi for family members and what not.

I'm getting up to go dispose of my food pack when my phone starts ringing, and I look down to see it's Jide calling me. He is impatient tonight because he didn't wait for me to call him.

I answer once out of earshot of my mum and her sisters.

"Jide, why are you so impatient today?"

I didn't even wait for him to say hello, and his response to my question is a low chuckle.

"I wanted to hear your voice, but then, I had this intense need also to see you before I went to bed."

Thank God, I am alone in the kitchen or whoever sees my face right now would know that I am talking to Jide, because he always knows how to put a big smile on my face, ever the charmer.

"That's easy, Jide. You know we could video chat. It won't hurt also to see your face."

"I've got a better solution to our need this night. I don't know how, but I ended up driving to your house."

"What?"

"Sewa, I'm downstairs. Please grace me with your presence."

"You can't be serious."

"Dead-serious."

"Jide, I know we have a thing going on between us, but you can't just show up unannounced. It's not proper."

"But Sewa, you can't announce surprises. Please, can we have this mini-argument in person, rather than on the phone when I'm a few feet away from you?"

I am more than thrilled that he is outside. This is the kind of surprise I love, but there is a need for some boundaries if we don't want to end up choking each other. I quietly make my way out of the apartment.

Jide is parked in front of the gate of the building and is resting his back on the passenger door of his car. Once he sees me, a dazzling smile takes over his face, and that's when I remember what I am wearing. I am braless, in sleeping shorts and a tank top. Now the swaying of my free breasts feels more pronounced, and I grow self-conscious.

"I should pay you more nightly visits if this is how I'm going to find you."

"Shut up, Jide. You better not come without telling me first again."

"Yes, ma. Now can I hug you? I've missed you."

He doesn't wait for my response before sweeping me into his arms and pressing my front to his. I'm wrapped in him and enveloped by his scent. This is easily becoming my happiest place to be.

I break away from him not long after because I can feel the curious eyes staring at our public display of affection, and I know it won't be long before I am the talk of our estate. Jide and I sit in the back of his car with the A/C and backlight on, and we are given a bit of privacy because his car glasses are tinted.

We end up kissing the minutes away like horny teenagers. Ever since the wedding, anytime Jide and I have been alone, we somehow end up lip-locked. I break away from our kiss and push him away from me.

"Jide, I didn't tell my mum where I was going. I should go back inside."

"Sewa, I swear I've never been as taken with anyone as I am with you."

"Hmph. You that my friends think you've used jazz for me, the way I just light up when I see your name or you're being spoken about."

Jide laughs at my response, but it's true that I'm equally taken with him. He is holding my hand, and I love his touch—it's soothing and feels right.

"What do you say to us making our relationship official?"

"It wasn't official before?" I say, not wanting to give away how happy I am that he is ready to define our relationship. He might claim I am his woman to the whole world, but it's never right to just assume and go with the flow. I always preach that people have to define their relationships, discuss, and communicate with each other what exactly they want or are to each other, for the other not to be left behind.

"It has always been official to me, Sewa, but it's time we speak about us and the future of our relationship because I want a future with you."

I'm about to tell him how much I want that, too, when a loud knock on the front window of his car startles us.

It's no other than my mum and her sisters, ha! Aye mi temi bami! Oh, lord, I am in trouble. These women have brought their problem downstairs. I will never see the end of this.

"Jide, see what you have caused now? My nosey aunts and Mum have come to find me."

"Baby, it's not that serious jo. Why are you acting like you're still a small child that has been caught doing something bad? Besides, I am your boyfriend, and I am doing nothing wrong. After all, I'm parked in front of your home. It's not like I am dragging you off somewhere to do wonderful things to you in private."

"You're my boyfriend?"

"Of course. Do you disagree? If you disagree, I could be more than your boyfriend to you. Just say the word, baby."

I laugh at his response, and he quickly pecks me on my nearest cheek before opening the car door and allowing me to get down from his car to face my elders. He follows behind me; we are in this together.

Jide immediately prostrates in greeting as Yoruba tradition demands when in the presence of our elders and straightens up. My mum and her sisters nod in acknowledgement and answer his greetings, but they have an air of false anger surrounding them.

"Adesewa! To ri okunrin o ku ro ninu ile, o so fun wa pe o lo si isale! Ti a wa e ka kiri ni oke."

My mum starts scolding me immediately in Yoruba after she accepts Jide's greeting. But I can tell she's only mildly annoyed that I left and went downstairs to meet Jide, not just any man as she said, without announcing it.

"E ma binu ma. It's my fault. I held her back longer than I should have."

Jide begs them not to be angry as he defends my honour. I fight the urge to roll my eyes—I can stand my ground against my mum.

"Mummy, I'm sorry. I should have said so, but it was because I was going downstairs, that's why, and you could have called me on the phone."

My mum throws me a scathing look, but I don't balk. I know this is just an excuse to bring her sisters to see my boyfriend.

"Aunties Jumoke and Jola, this is Jide, my boyfriend. I'm so sorry I caused you people distress. Jide and I were about to come upstairs to greet you."

My aunts start making ridiculous noises as they begin washing both me and Jide in prayers. Once they stop and are satisfied I am in one piece, they decide to leave us alone again finally, but my mum asks that we come inside instead of staying out, which we kindly reject as Jide announces he has to be going soon, but another time, he surely would.

This time around, we don't enter into the backseat of his car. Instead, I follow him around and watch him settle himself in the driver seat. He turns off the backlight of his car, and I lean against his seating position as I stand. The moonlight is illuminating our faces.

"We have always been official, but I'm glad we are both on the same page," I announce before kissing him.

I love kissing him. His arms wrap around my waist, and I can't help but smile into the kiss.

"Sewa, Mummy is calling you!"

I groan, and we both break away from the kiss laughing. His arms pull me closer to him before he releases me. I say goodbye and watch him drive away, before turning to face my brother who is standing at the entrance of the gate of our building smirking because he knows he had interrupted me.

"Sewa, see don't beat me o! Abeg, it was Mummy that sent me."

CHAPTER NINE

I am nervous. It's going to be my first time taking the floor at a client meeting which includes all the heads of the company and team members working on this project with me as well as the author whose book covers and interior I designed. I will be explaining how and why I went with the designs I used and how it complements the story the book is trying to tell.

I love how everything turned out, the book front and back covers, the spine and the interior. I know the author will also love it as much as I do. I am a nervous wreck because, not only is it going to be my first time taking the floor, but it's also my first solo assignment, so I have to prove to them that hiring me was not a mistake.

The book, *Sinister*, is about twin sisters, Taiwo and Kehinde, who grew up in an abusive home. There was no love lost between their parents, and they watched as one of their father's jilted mistresses murdered their parents before taking her own life. The twist is that their upbringing and experiencing such trauma at a young age has its consequences, especially when left untreated. One of the sisters, Kehinde, becomes a murderer and is out for blood due to pent-up anger and resentment she held inside, and it's only Taiwo that can stop or find her.

It's one hell of a crazy plot and a remarkable story to read. I was instantly captivated, and designing the graphics for this book made me so proud and giddy inside. This story not only needs kickass covers and graphics, but it also deserves it. I love working in the book industry.

"I don't understand why you're nervous. You know you've got this in the bag already."

I startle as Dieko breaks my inner musing; I am that lost in my head, I did not even notice him enter the kitchen where I am helping myself to a soothing cup of hot cocoa. Taking the seat beside me, he is looking at me with amusement.

"I know I've got it, but it's first-time jitters. I'll be fine once I get into stride."

"You killed the graphics for *Sinister*, and you more than blew me away. You're pure talent. No one can argue you're not. With this pep talk said, you should be on your way there now, seeing as Mrs. Anobi just left her office and is on her way up."

Shoot! I down what's left of my drink in one gulp and deposit my mug in the sink, then grab my meeting essentials—flash drive, notepad, and pen—before speed-walking to the elevator, with Dieko and James' combined laughter echoing after me.

I thankfully am not the last to arrive, nor has the meeting started or is about to begin. It starts a cool seven minutes after I take a seat beside Mrs. Anobi, the head of my department.

Once our client, the author, walks in and settles down, the meeting starts.

Recently, I have not been as clumsy and accident-prone as I usually am. Which is the cause of my mistake, for I should have taken it as the sign it was. My great streak coming to a tragic end. Whenever things are going so high and nothing terrible is happening at all, it's a warning something awful is to occur. Well, it's a warning for me, but there I was being too blissfully happy to take note of the signs, until after I tripped over nothing as I headed to the front of the room, where I was to be presenting.

I don't know why it happened; I'm still trying to understand. One second, I am walking fine in my sensible, low-heeled shoes, and the next, I am falling knee-first to the floor. The sound effects my fall drew from the people in the room were so dramatic, I couldn't help but smile and laugh in embarrassment, wishing the ground would claim me and make me disappear.

The floor obviously didn't grant my wish, and so, I was assisted up and checked to be sure I was fine before the meeting was restored as I was given a few seconds to collect myself and recover before I start my presentation.

Despite the small mishap before I started, I nail my presentation. The author and everyone could not keep their awe inside. My head felt like it was going to detach itself from my neck, because of how inflated my ego got from all the praise about my creative mind and skills I received.

As embarrassing as my fall was when it happened, I know sharing the story will bring about laughter, and so I shared it. I recounted my tragic occurrence to my co-workers, friends, and family. They all laughed except my mum who asked if I was okay, before proceeding to lecture me on posture and the proper way of walking. Mothers.

Jide laughed the loudest and longest, I could not believe him. He really wished he was there to see me go down, which set off another round of laughter before he said, still laughing his pants off, "I'm not always going to be there to comfort you afterwards."

This, of course, thrilled me. I couldn't be more glad he wasn't there because as far as I am concerned, he has had his quota of seeing me awkwardly falling or walking into things.

I'm at the dining eating my dinner when I hear my phone's ringtone getting louder by the second as Demola comes into view holding it.

"Sewa, Nnoli is calling you."

I snatch my phone from his hand and look at him sternly. What was he looking for in my room?

"If anything is missing inside my room, I'm coming for you," I warn him then quickly answer Nnoli's call before my phone stops ringing.

"Hey, baby girl."

"Don't baby girl me, Nnoli. Do you think I'll just forget how you and the others just finished teasing me?"

"You're not serious. That was over an hour ago, and you're still butt hurt."

"Really? Oya why are you calling me?"

"I can't call you again ni?"

"Sorry ma. Please, why are you calling me?"

"Good gi—"

"Nnoli if I catch you."

"Ahn, somebody cannot play with you again."

"Abeg jo."

"Okay o, Sewa. This weekend, we are all available, so I was thinking, isn't it time for us, your friends, to meet Jide, at least before your mum's wedding?"

"Can you imagine? They nominated you for the meet-the-boyfriend talk."

"It's true, though. Your friends are meant to meet your boyfriend before he meets your parents, but not only has Jide met your mum more than once may I add, he has also met Mr. Saludeen and your brother."

"Fine. I'll talk to him and get back to you guys about it."

"You better, and he should better be prepared, 'coz we girls aren't going to take it easy on him. Especially with how you both have gotten serious so quick."

"I know, right. Nnoli, it's surprising even to me how fast I am falling for him, but I have no worries, because I know when you girls meet him, you all will like him."

"Stop right there, Mrs. I am in love. We can make our own opinion of him ourselves, you don't need to convince us."

I roll my eyes and loudly kiss my teeth, because why can girlfriends be so rude but yet you can feel the love for you rooted in the rudeness?

"Whatever, Nnoli! Oya can I go back to my food?"

"Yes, bye, love."

"Bye jo."

I end the call and focus on my food, which is now getting cold. I have only taken four spoons when Demola meekly approaches me, and I roll my eyes inwardly. What does he want from me now, or what has he done? Before he can open his mouth, I ask him.

"What?"

"Why are you angry? I just wanted to ask if you wanted me to go and charge your phone for you."

There is something suspicious going on, if he is offering to help me, without me asking him to. I hand him my phone, and he gladly takes it from my hand, but before he is off, I ask him again.

"What did you do or what do you want?"

"Nothing, I'm just a good brother."

"Na so o! When you're ready, you'll come and meet me."

Demola just smiles at me, and there is something off about it. Let whatever it is he wants or has done not let my blood boil because the little brat has been nothing but mischievous playing his stupid pranks on me.

I call Jide as soon as I get back to my room and inform him of the meetup with my girlfriends. I try to find a way out of us going, hinting that he has work and other events that need his presence and attention this weekend, but he brushes me off. I am not eager because knowing these girls, they plan to ambush him. I would have preferred it if I was the one who brought it up because then, the meeting would be in my control.

But instead of picking up on my not-so-subtle hints, Jide ignores me and jumps at the opportunity. In fact, he sounds very enthusiastic as he calmly tells me I have nothing to worry about because my friends will love him and because he's just that likeable. If I was asked about a month ago who had the largest ego amongst the people in my life, I would have proudly proclaimed "I do!" I didn't know my future boyfriend was coming to outshine me.

I tell my friends the apparent good news via one of our many group chats. They didn't even wait for a confirmation from me as they had already started planning for the meet-up.

Seeing as it is the time of the month again for our mandatory monthly get-together, they decided this would one should be a special event, because they went as far as titling it 'Meeting Sewa's Newest Boyfriend.' Onyinyechi will be hosting us all at her apartment on Saturday. All we have to do is set the menu for the night, dividing the eating and drinking provisions for the meet-up amongst ourselves.

I beg Nafisa to bring Sani along on the day because I know Sani will bring a sort of balance and the girls won't go all out on Jide because they'll also subject Sani a bit to their outrageous treatment which has now become our tradition. Sani was the first to receive it when Nafisa got serious about her feelings for him. Followed by

Onyinyechi's then-love interest, which gratefully did not last—something was off about the man. Nnoli hasn't shown deep interest in anyone yet, but I think she's purposely hiding whoever it is that has captured her attention because there are signs of there being a lover in her life, or I may just be trying too hard to see something when there is nothing.

Because I dread the upcoming weekend, time becomes a nasty joke, for before I know it, the day called 'Meeting Sewa's Newest Boyfriend' has arrived.

One full week has gone by since Jide became officially my boyfriend, and he's already so comfortable in my home, conversing with any of my available family members, either my mum, her fiancé, or my brother. Twice this week, he picked me up after work, and he also comes to visit me whenever we are both free—which is at night during the week. We go out for dinner or we don't go out and eat dinner with my family, with the latter being more than the first.

When I conceded that I am his girlfriend, it changed things for the better because now, he knows he has the right to do so. I'm not complaining because I've seen him almost every single day since then, and the more I get to know him, the harder I fall for him.

'Meet Sewa's Newest Boyfriend' commences at five o'clock in the evening. Since I'm in charge of drinks and desserts, I'm meant to get there on time, to preserve the food and get the drinks moderately chilled before it's time to consume them. Instead, I purposely finish getting ready by five on the dot and drag Jide out of my home so that we can be on our way. My home to Onyinyechi's house is about forty minutes without traffic, so I know it will give the others plenty of time to arrive before us since I live the farthest from Onyinyechi.

We are the last to arrive. I leave Jide to fend for himself since he claims to have everything under control, and I rush to hug Nafisa because she listened to me. Sani is here, sitting on a couch watching TV. He smiles as he shakes his head at me, apparently knowing why I'm extra happy to see Nafisa.

I release Nafisa from my hold to introduce her to Jide, but he's not in the room. Sani says he's in the kitchen, and that's where Nafisa and I find him, talking to both Nnoli and Onyinye. The strangest thing, though, is they all have smiles on their faces and look like they are old friends, not people who just met each other.

Once I'm by his side again, he wraps his arm around my back and draws me closer to him, not breaking his conversation.

"Jide, these are my friends. Onyinyechi, Nnoli, and Nafisa. And the guy on the sofa is Sani, Nafisa's fiancé."

Jide turns to face Nafisa with a massive smile on his face. I look over at her, and I know she's trying her hardest not to smile just as widely at him. His personality and aura draw people in and captivate them.

"Congratulations on your engagement. I'm so glad I can finally meet Sewa's friends. She speaks highly of you all. Let me leave you ladies to yourselves and introduce myself to your fiancé."

With that, he calmly excuses himself from our presence. All eyes are on me, and I can't help the huge smile on my face. Everyone else looks amused at my reaction, and I just shrug at them.

"I like him. He seems smart and like a wise guy. Judging from the little introductory talk we had," Onyinye announces, but that's Onyinyechi for you. She likes people quickly.

The hard part is her now letting you in as a friend. Most people think Onyinyechi considers them a friend, because of her bubbly and open persona. But even though she's open, she's still closed off, and only a few people really get to see the real her, and that's when her full personality shines through.

Nnoli nods in agreement, and Nafisa shakes her head at them, saying they are falling prey to his natural charm, making me laugh. The verdict on him is still undecided—that's the conclusion they fall on, for the first interaction, but I'm positive now that Jide is going to make them all swoon. We set about transferring the various food and snacks from their containers into bowls and plates, to be placed on the dining table, ready to start our evening.

CHAPTER TEN

When Jide says he's got it, he truly means it, and I know now not to worry. 'Meet Sewa's Newest Boyfriend' went off without a hitch, and Jide's connection with my best friends is only getting stronger with each day since their official meeting. I mean, the rude people now have a new message group on WhatsApp that includes Jide but excludes me, which I find very weird. It isn't normal when your boyfriend and your best friends have discussions together, purposely leaving you out. They also find it hilarious, sharing titbits of their conversations with me, such as screenshots.

I dread going home after work. I want to stay as far away from home as possible because it has turned into Party Central. Mum and Mr. Saludeen are officially getting married on Friday, at the marriage registry at Ikoyi, but last-minute preparations are currently ongoing since the wedding party is being held this Saturday. The buzz in the air, the stream of family members, friends, and guests, is never-ending, and the apartment has become insufferable.

It's all too much for me. I can't wait for peace when Mum, Mr. Saludeen, and Demola go away for the summer. To the point that I am very thankful for my workload which has doubled because of how much people were raving and loving the cover and design for *Sinister* at its official cover unveiling. Now, a lot of authors have requested for me to create the perfect designs and covers for their books. Many of these authors are also approaching me to do freelance work as they are not under *Palm and Co.*, so I am making extra money for doing what I love.

Today is another milestone for me and Jide's relationship because he is picking me up after work, and our destination is his house at Ogudu GRA, where he is going to cook us a meal and for us to unwind from the day.

This is a big deal because this is the first time I am going to his place and also the first time we would be completely alone in the course of our relationship.

I was complaining to him about how stressed brainstorming for the perfect idea and bringing it to life was making me, the extracurricular activities that were going on at home not helping, so I was wary of going home immediately after work. That's how he offered to take me to his house and pamper me, and I readily agreed.

I have been leaving the office late since my workload increased last week, so when Dieko doesn't drop me off or Jide doesn't come to get me, I use Bolt to get home because it's not safe for me to be using public transport or being out by myself late at night. Thanks to all the work I'm getting, I can start saving to buy myself a car, and at this rate, in a year, I will be able to.

The ringtone I set for Jide sounds out from my phone—he has arrived. I pick up his call while starting to pack up my things and shutting off all the electronic appliances.

"Hey, baby, I'm here."

"Hi, babe. I'll be down in less than five."

"Sewa, I told you I was almost here five minutes ago. You workaholic."

"See this pot calling kettle black. Jide, talking to you is slowing me down. You're extremely impatient, and I'm only a few feet away from you."

"A few feet too far, baby."

I laugh and end the call a smile on my face. Once I've turned off everything, I grab my bags and lock my office door. On my way down, being the chicken that I am, I shoot off a text to my mum, that I won't be coming home early because I'm going out with Jide tonight. I know if I call her, she might start questioning me about my whereabouts or even give me sexual advice on using protection or what not. I'm just not in the mood for any of her shenanigans tonight.

"Good night, madam."

I smile and return the greeting to Mr. Baker, one of the security guards working here. I step out of the building, and the first thing I see is Jide and his car. He is waiting to open the front passenger door for me, ever the chivalrous one. He remains where he is as I approach, and when I'm in front of him, he takes my laptop bag from me and plants a chaste kiss on my lips before opening the door for me to enter. He closes the door and deposits my laptop bag on the back seat before making his way to the driver side and gets in.

"How was your day?" he asks as he starts the car and drives us out the gates of my workplace.

I watch him, taking in his presence. He looks sexily dishevelled, his tie removed, some buttons undone, and shirt untucked. He looks so calm and at ease, like he has not a single worry in the world as he easily controls his car.

"Sewa, is all well? You've not answered me. Do you not want to go to my place again? It's no pressure. We can go elsewhere."

"What? Jide, abeg calm down jo. I was just checking you out. You don't know how being near you affects the way I think."

The smile that lights up his faces warms me immediately. I did not mean to say the last part, but it just came out of my mouth, instead of staying inside my mind. He takes a hand away from the steering wheel and takes hold of my left one and squeezes it.

"I am so thankful and happy you came crashing into my life, Sewa. Ever since we met, I've felt nothing but happiness, and my life feels complete with you in it."

"This is starting to start like a marriage proposal, Jide. My day was good but busy, and it's about to get better because you're cooking for me."

"You can act like you don't feel what I feel between us, Sewa, but I know you do, so keep playing and deceiving yourself."

"Haba Jide! Me deceiving myself? I'm just realistic. I feel happy also and everything you just said. My life is on the right track as of now, and I couldn't be more pleased, but it's still so new. We still have so many hurdles to jump over, which I more than look forward to, but there's no need for us to rush."

"But who says I'm rushing? It's okay if you're not ready, but I know how I feel. But I'll set that aside for now. What will my dearest like for me to cook for her?"

"I don't know. Surprise me."

He laughs at that. We chat all the way to his place, and not once does he release my hand from his. The bout of emotions Jide stirs up, I can feel it in every atom of my being, and it's making me so scared because I think it might be love.

He takes me on a tour of his elegant, yet simple house. A three-storey building, which I think is too big for a bachelor. He says he bought it for his future family, and he got it at a reasonable price. He hired an interior decorator to design his home, so everything matches— it's a modern minimalist look that works, and I fall so in love. On the ground floor, there is the entry foyer, a guest toilet, a living room with a connecting dining room, which also leads to the kitchen and two bedrooms, with a spiral stairway leading upstairs. The first floor has three bedrooms, a living room, and a small room that's half the size of a bedroom. The final storey has only one staircase leading into it, and I know it's Jide's personal space.

It's a suite, which is housing a spacious veranda. In a corner is his bedroom, accommodating his massive king-size bed. Bedside drawers flank the sides, a couch and a furry rug are in front of the bed facing a huge TV set, speakers and what not on the wall opposite the bed. He has a walk-in closet, which I am sure he can never fill with all his clothes, and his bathroom has a walk-in shower, a freaking jacuzzi, bidet, toilet, and a double basin, with cupboards under them. There's a built-in shelf with different racks that are holding stacks of folded towels, air fresheners, toilet cleaning and bathroom supplies, and rolls of tissue paper.

In another corner, there is a study which resembles a mini-office. The wall opposite it is stacked with three shelves from top to bottom, and one out of three is brimming with books. There are comfortable-looking couches for reading in front of it, and a small table that divides the shelves and couches.

There is also a small dining table for four along one corner, which looks like a mini-kitchen. There's a two-door, two-in-one fridge and freezer, which produces water and ice, and marble-top-surface cupboards with a steel basin for washing things at its middle. On one side of the marble top sits a microwave, a kettle, and at the opposite side, a rack of plates, bowls, cups, and necessary kitchen utensils.

"You went all out for your room. It's a house in a house!" is the first thing that leaves my mouth once I take everything in.

Jide is far away lounging on a sofa, resting as he watches me with amusement on his face. I remove my shoes as I walk towards him and deposit myself on top of him. He lets out a huff and draws me closer to him, so my head is resting on his chest as I stretch my body on top of his. His hand goes to wrap around my back, to hug our bodies together. I look up at him to find him already smiling down at me.

"Jide, I don't feel like moving or eating anymore."

"Too bad. I brought you here to feed you, so you're going to have to eat, eventually, because I like where I am right now."

I relax my body and rest my head comfortably on his chest, just listening to his heartbeat. His house is very overwhelming because it's now really hitting me how rich and well-off Jide is. He owns Druin, so of course he's rich, but the extent and enormity of it all is really dawning on me now. It's making feel some way, but I push the negativity aside, because to hell with it. I may try to deny it, but I know I love Jide regardless of who he is, and I suspect he knows it.

"Why don't you ever talk about your dad?"

I'm so surprised by his question, I have to sit up, still on him, so that I can look him well in the face. I think back to all our conversations, and it's true I've never once mentioned my dad, and he has never asked, so I did not have a reason to talk about him.

"My dad died ten years ago. He was a good father. I have some happy memories about my childhood with him in it. But he was a terrible husband and man in general. I thought I had told you."

"I'm sorry. Hopefully, he's in a better place now."

"I doubt it, Jide. He was a true Yoruba demon, abusive in every way to my mum. My mum needed to get away from him. I remember how afraid she was back then. We had to sneak out of the house in the dead of night to escape him. She didn't even know she was pregnant, and because she feared he would take Demola from her when he was born, she never gave him the opportunity to meet his son. When he died, his death really shook her, and she took it the hardest and I think it's because the weight of the guilt she felt for keeping his son away from him crushed her."

Jide doesn't speak once I'm through talking. He just calmly stares at me. The mood in the room is sombre, and I think he seems sad. I just shrug at him, about to say something to lighten the mood, when he stops me.

Instead, he sits up and moves me until I am sitting on his lap. He looks at me and smiles reassuringly before his arms wrap around my back and pull me until we are hugging each other. It's a while before we release ourselves.

"Come on, let's go downstairs. It's time to eat."

I let out a disgruntled groan, but Jide is already pushing me up so he can get up also. Once standing, he grabs me by the waist and carries me in his arms, spinning us around and making me squeal. I immediately start pleading for him to set me back on my feet. Which he doesn't do immediately, and when he finally does, he makes sure there isn't any space between us two as he keeps an arm locked around my waist.

"You know that I'm only going to do right by you? And if I ever hurt you, it will be unintentional, and I'll make up for it. Sewa, I'm a sure thing, and you never have to doubt when it comes to us or me."

I look up at him, and his face is as serious as it can ever be, which makes my heart pound with happiness because I feel his words everywhere and I just want to melt into a puddle at his feet as my body overheats with the storm of feelings he has awakened inside my soul.

"Jide, please kiss me, before I combust."

He laughs and starts for my lips, granting me my desire, and the love I feel fills up my heart so much, I fear it's going to burst. I don't wait for his lips to reach mine and go for it. I kiss him with everything in me, and I hope he can feel how much I love him from this kiss.

"Please, can we leave my room now? I don't think it's safe for both of us right now if we don't want to give in to delicious temptation. I especially can't ravish you as much as I want to when I still have to return you home."

"What makes you think the kitchen would stop us?"

We leave and are heading down for to the main kitchen when the power goes off, leaving us in total darkness. This is so funny to me, I start laughing out loud because in a place this grand, you would think there is always power, forgetting that no matter where in Nigeria, the power will surely go off certain times in a day.

"Why are you laughing?"

"I'm just surprised that NEPA took your power."

"You know we aren't on government property, right? Don't worry sha, the generator will be on any second now. By the way, NEPA doesn't exist anymore."

"You and I know that I know that, but it's never going to stop the majority of Nigerian's cursing NEPA whenever the power is gone."

We randomly discuss as we continue making our way to his kitchen. By the time we get there, his generator is on, and the power in his home is restored.

CHAPTER ELEVEN

The first people to wish me happy birthday are my mum, Demola, Mr. Saludeen, and Nosirat, our house help. Lucky for us, we are having a peaceful night at home, nobody but us—the residents who rightfully live in the apartment are indoors.

They sing and pray for me before each of them hand over presents they have gotten me, Demola and Nosirat included, which surprises me because neither of them has ever given me anything before, but they both know how to collect things from me.

Mum and Mr. Saludeen got me clothes, a perfume, and a boxed set of soaps and lotions for my birthday. Demola gives me five thousand naira, which I'm sure Mr. Saludeen gave him, because he doesn't know how to save money, not to talk about him actually gifting me money, and finally, Nosirat gives me a purse. I thank them profusely for their gifts to me and after that, because my phone wouldn't stop ringing in order to give me privacy to answer my callers, they don't stay in my room for long.

The girls call me via group call. Which I was expecting, allowing them to share their greetings at the same time, promising me that we would all hang out soon, so they can treat me for my birthday and hand over the presents they have for me.

After the girls' call came many more calls but none from Jide. I thought he had fallen asleep and wouldn't have held it against him, but once the calls stopped coming in, I noticed the message he sent me.

Jide: I had given up on ever finding my soul-mate, but I was wrong because I have you now. Each day that goes by with you in it makes my world a happy place and I never want to lose that. I know you're going to be so popular tonight, I've been trying to call but... See you when you wake up. Happy birthday, baby

I don't reply his text or anyone else's. Instead, I go to sleep and wake up at my usual time to get ready for work. Because it is my birthday doesn't give me a pass to be late for work. I am on my phone finally replying all the texts I got before I slept, heading to the living room, when I get a whiff of perfume that comes along with Jide Harriman. When I see him, it immediately sets my heart beating in a frenzy.

That's what he meant when he said *see you when you wake up.* I had my suspicions that he was going to come take me to work today, but here he is, earlier than ever, comfortably sitting on his favourite couch. Once he spies me, I watch as his face lights up. He gets up and immediately engulfs me in a full body hug before lightly pecking me on my lips.

"Happy birthday, baby. I made you breakfast."

If it was possible for me to melt, I would long ago have found a home in a bottle he took everywhere him. Instead, I capture his mouth and kiss him again. I am not worried about anyone finding me kissing him as if he was my life-line because my family members sleep in until nine a.m. earliest, especially when they have no reason to be up early.

"My father used to cook, when he wanted to apologize for doing something wrong. I hated it when he cooked, because it meant my mum was hiding at her friend's place after they had fought over something and he had badly bruised her."

"Sewa, I am so sorry you had to experience that when you were so little. I would like to know why you're telling me this now."

"It's just, you cooked for me, and it's a beautiful thing, but it also made me remember, especially now that my mum is getting married again tomorrow, all these memories. The good, the bad, and the ugly keep resurfacing, but ultimately, I am so relieved and happy that she will never experience such brutality from Mr. Saludeen's hands, and what they have between them is so pure and true."

"I'll drink to their happily ever after, and Sewa, you know I'm here for you always, whenever you need to talk."

I nod, because I know deep down he is also as good as Mr. Saludeen is inside. I take his face in my hands and press a kiss to each of his cheeks, an affectionate thank you, before I pick up my fork to start eating.

After we both devour the food which he made for two so he could eat with me, we leave my home as he is also taking me to my office. On the way, he informs me of our night plans for the day, claiming I have to clock out from work early and go home, to change and get dolled up for the evening, because he has a treat he wants me to have for my birthday.

My birthday is much more dramatic than I expect because it becomes an office event. Three cakes. From the management, my department, and Jide. The author of *Sinister* caters small chops to everyone in the office, and Jide also had chilled drinks delivered for everyone in the firm. I got lots of gifts from various people I have befriended and some authors that I've designed books for. An outsider would believe I am a visiting celebrity.

The shower of love I have been receiving from the second the time read 00:00 A.M. is so breath-taking. I can't remember any other birthday of mine that surpassed this one, although it could be, because of the fact that I have more people in my life than I did before now.

Jide hires a driver to get me home after work, and I can't be more thankful because I have too many things and presents to carry home. For the first time ever, I am closing exactly at five p.m. and no one even tries to stop me. In fact, they kindly wave me off with good wishes.

It's surprising how the apartment is empty, with no guest or wedding party planners. I mean, Mr. Saludeen and Mum are going to the marriage registry to officially get married tomorrow, and the day after tomorrow is for their wedding party. I'm expecting chaos and what not in the house, like it has been the previous days of this week, but it is eerily calm and collected.

Mum looks as if she just came back from a party with Mr. Saludeen, and Demola is lying on a couch, eyes glued to the movie that is being shown on the TV.

"You're home early, Sewa. Is all well?" Mum asks as she and Mr. Saludeen watch in amusement as Nosirat, Yusuf the gateman, and I carry everything I brought with me from the office into the apartment. I carried Jide's cake home and shared the other two with the people at work.

"Yes, Mum. I was instructed by Jide to come and change into something nice, because he is treating me to an outing tonight as a present."

"How was your day at the office?"

"It was so wonderful, Mummy. So many people gave me things and wished me a happy birthday."

I continue to tell her about my day, and she is preening at the fact that so many people like me in my office. I know she is thinking about how all the home training she has beaten into me is finally paying off for the better.

I excuse myself to take a shower and get ready because Jide said he'll be here by seven p.m. and we have to be on our way exactly five minutes after if we want to meet the reservation for seven-thirty that he got for us. If he is trying to be secretive about where he is taking me, he is failing dreadfully, because it can only be a high-end, fine-dining restaurant he is taking me to if he is worried about promptly meeting the reservation.

I have this sexy dress I've been saving for a special occasion, a white, strappy, open-back midi dress. It's both sexy and elegant, and I love it. With only forty-five minutes left before Jide arrives, I proceed to apply the most natural-looking nude makeup on my face and I'm done with ten minutes to spare, which I use to take selfies and post on my social networking channels and reply my happy birthday well-wishers.

Five minutes to seven, Jide messages me that he has arrived and is heading up. My family did not move from the living room in the time it took me to get ready, and when my mum sees me, she's up and fluttering around me, telling me how pretty I look and urging me to pose so she can take my picture.

I basically push Jide out of the door after he greets my family, reminding him and them that we have a reservation to meet. He laughs and willingly allows me to draw him out of the apartment so we can be on our way.

Twenty minutes into the journey, his phone starts ringing. He looks at the caller and immediately picks the call via his Bluetooth device, eyes on the road. I watch as his facial expression changes from indifferent to anger, speaking in clipped tones. Once he ends the call, he faces me, wearing a look of apology.

"Sewa, something of importance just came up. One of my clients is demanding to see me and is threatening to sue if I don't show up because apparently, one of my trusted employees made a money-losing error in the application we made for him."

"That's tough, Jide. What's going to happen now?"

"I first need to drop by home to get some files, then get to the office. I'm so sorry I'm ruining your day, but I assure you it wouldn't take up to an hour and we'll be off again. I'll make another reservation elsewhere for us."

"We don't have to go out again, and I can just go home. I've had a long, pleasant day. It's okay you have work, especially since it's a legal issue."

"No, you're not backing out. I was thinking I could drop you off at my home instead. I love the thought of you being in my home, a lot more than dropping you off at your home."

I blush, and his face warms up with the smile he throws my way. I nod in agreement. The volume of his smile increases at my acceptance. In fact, he seems too happy for someone who might be about to be issued a lawsuit.

It takes forty minutes to get to his house. He leads me inside while he apologises again for messing up our plans for the night and delaying it a bit. I really don't understand why he is apologising—some things can't be helped, and this is such a situation.

"It's enough o Jide. I've heard jo."

"Okay, Sewa, I just don't like disappointing you."

He opens the door into his house, and once we reach the entrance of the foyer leading to the living room, the lights in his house automatically come on, as well as the voluminous chorus of "Surprise!" that greets me. I scream and move backwards in fear into Jide, who laughs near my ear and whispers his own surprise into it.

People are recording me as they laugh at my reaction to the surprise, which I was not expecting at all. I turn around and hug Jide before letting him go. I spy my mischievous girlfriends, who come and pull me into a group hug. Once they release me, they put a birthday girl sash on me and a crown, which is very corny, but I love them, so I wear their gifts gladly.

There are so many people in attendance. Mine and Jide's friends, people from the office, my aunties, Mum and Mr. Saludeen, Demola and my cousins, with some young kids I've never seen before. I go and greet and thank my aunties for showing up and also to go and meet my mum because I can't believe they actually pulled off a surprise party for me. No wonder they didn't complain too much when I dragged Jide from the apartment earlier.

It was Jide's idea, Nafisa gladly dishes as she and the girls inform me while we eat delicious ice cream. The group chat they created was used mostly to plan the event and making sure I wasn't aware, and everything went off without a hitch. They had not been too sure about Jide being able to pull this whole thing off by keeping it a secret and getting me to his home on time, but now we all know that Jide's acting skills are impeccable.

I receive more gifts from people in attendance. My friends quip about giving me my gift today also making sense as they all knew they would have seen me today. They wouldn't let me open the gifts and told me to save it for later, building up my curiosity.

I notice Jide walk in with two older people I do not know or have ever met. They are laughing at something he says as if he knows I'm watching him. He looks at me, and the people, noticing he isn't paying attention, also follow his line of sight to me. Then he turns to them and obviously starts talking about me to them. He looks at me and nods before he leads them to where my mum, Mr. Saludeen, and aunties are sitting.

He introduces them, and everyone gets up to hug each other, and I widen my eyes at him. He takes that as his cue to come to me.

"What is going on, Jide?"

"I have people to introduce you to. They are dying to meet you."

He cannot be serious right now. Why is he doing this right now? He didn't even let me be prepared. Instead, he ambushes me with another surprise at my own freaking surprise party. He notices the look I am giving him—I bet my eyes are very wide and alarmed because I suddenly feel very nervous and shy.

"Come on, Sewa. My parents don't bite."

He invited his parents. I am about to meet his parents. Who springs a surprise meet-the-parents at one's surprise birthday party?

CHAPTER TWELVE

I don't know what planet Jide's brain lives on, because it isn't on the same one with the rest of us. This has to be the case because I can't think of any other reason that would have led him to believe it's okay to surprise me with meeting his parents.

His parents were very warm and welcoming. They set my nervous self at ease once Jide introduced me to them and his mother embraced me. Before she and her husband wished me a happy birthday, they also insisted they were the ones who made Jide invite them, because they couldn't wait to meet me, and this party was the perfect opportunity. We made our way to my mum, who took it upon herself to make them as comfortable and as welcomed as possible in the mist of unfamiliar faces. I love my mum so much.

Once they were settled, I dragged Jide away to castigate him for not giving me any sort of warning, regardless of the fact that the party was a surprise party. He didn't say anything and only smiled at me while looking sheepish until I finished my tirade, and then he proceeded to hug me and said he won't let go until I hugged him back. While we were embracing each other, he kissed me on the forehead and released me.

"You're not going to say anything, Jide?"

"No, because it's not a big deal. My parents just want to meet their future daughter-in-law."

"First of all, we aren't engaged. Neither of us proposed or ever discussed marriage. Also, how do you know I won't say no if you propose?"

"I just know. It's you or no one else for me, Sewa. So I'll wait until whenever you're ready. I'll never stop asking as long as you still want me."

By the time he finished speaking, I was blushing, and my heart was beating so fast, I was speechless because this conversation had changed everything. This conversation was him telling me his expectations of our future and I blurted out, "I love you. I've known for a while now."

"I know you do because I love you just as much."

For the rest of the night, Jide did not leave my side, and I also did not want him to. Our parents and friends teased us mercilessly, but nothing could bring us down from the high our unplanned confession had brought us.

I loved my party, and everyone else had fun. Jide's mum exchanged contacts with me and my mum, who also invited his parents to her wedding. I personally thanked my best friends and everyone who came. Jide and the girls had prepared goodie bags filled with a small non-alcoholic wine bottle, a pack of gum, a unisex wallet, and a hand sanitizer for people who came to the party.

Everyone had good things to say about Jide and how they were hearing wedding bells in our future, but I chose not to respond to any of their assumptions. My birthday was the last day of work for the rest of the week for me, because I had to get ready and prepared for the wedding party on Saturday, plus my mum wanted me to be present at the marriage registry on Friday.

I was very happy for Mr. Saludeen and my mum. Once they signed everything and officially became a married couple in the eyes of the law, the glow of happiness and joy that they were exhibiting was so heart-warming to see.

The wedding party thankfully went off without any problem, and everyone seems happy and settled as they are seated in the reception hall, gladly conversing and taking pictures as loud music acts as the backdrop to the chatter of various conversations going on in the hall.

I, on the other hand, can't help but think back to my birthday night and when Jide and I said "I love you" to each other. It has had me floating on Cloud Nine, and it is helping in calming me down because my mum's wedding party is working my last nerve and I am trying really hard not to be upset.

I am frustrated, stressed, and tired. This is never a good combination for anyone when I get in this sort of mood as it brings out my snarky persona. Which makes it hard to act pleasant or be approachable when I'm on the edge of snapping.

I am so tired of greeting people and the number of my mother's friends who have called me to help them get something because as the child of the bride, I have access to everything.

I am very stressed because I can't leave. I am stuck here until the very end, and that is still hours away. Tosin and Demola have managed to dodge people, and I am getting the brunt of requests. I don't know where they have snuck off to, and the unfairness of it all is making my blood simmer.

The reason and cause of my unhappiness is Jide.

I haven't heard from him in over ten hours. Last I heard from him was a text message he had sent to me before I even woke up, about how he had an urgent matter to take care of and would be making a late appearance later in the day. I tried calling him immediately, wanting to know what was wrong, but his number was unreachable until it was switched off.

What really has me worried is he has not bothered to respond to any of the text messages I sent him, or anyone else's, for that matter.

His parents had arrived, expecting to see him here since they hadn't heard from him or been able to get a hold of him. Upon noticing my worry, his father tried reassuring me, asking me not to worry as he was sure Jide will contact us soon enough. I can tell they are slightly worried themselves because they are doing an average job of hiding it with positivity while trying to enjoy themselves. I can't enjoy myself as much as I want to because I am torn between being angry at him and worried about him.

I am seated with the girls, and we are all discussing anything and everything, in an effort to get me distracted enough, when Onyinyechi suddenly becomes silent. Unknown to Nafisa and Nnoli, I watch her as she builds up the nerve to say something important. She clears her throat loudly to capture the attention of the two of them once she sees I'm already looking at her.

"I found out yesterday that I am eight weeks pregnant."

Wow. I did not see that coming. She looks so vulnerable as she looks at us, waiting for us to speak our minds at her news.

"That's wonderful news, Onyinye!" Nafisa squeals, breaking the silence that we had unintentionally formed at her announcement because she really surprised us and we all had to digest the implications of her announcement.

I quickly followed after Nafisa finished speaking, and Nnoli also provided words of support after I spoke.

"Congratulations! I'm going to be Aunty Sewa sooner than I expected."

"Who is the baby father? You did not tell us you were seeing anyone. How could you not share with us, after all the trouble we have put on Sani and Jide?"

I laugh, but Nnoli is right. Onyinye has been keeping huge secrets from us. Despite her joyful news, she doesn't look as happy as she should be. In fact, her happy façade fell some more at Nnoli's question, and I know I am right to think something is wrong.

"He doesn't want to have anything to do with me. He told me to abort it or he'll leave. He said I should pick him or the thing inside me. I chose my baby."

I watch her eyes fill up with tears, and it breaks my heart. Nnoli is seated closest to her, so she instantly hugs her. Onyinye doesn't let the tears fall but blinks them away. We are all sombre now, and I'm about to speak when Nafisa starts speaking.

"Well, screw the idiot! Onyinye, you don't need him when you have us. This baby isn't just your baby. It's our baby, the four of us. This baby is going to grow up with so much love and support because our baby is going to be raised by four strong and independent women who have the most loving family and support system around them."

I nod in agreement as Nnoli also verbally agrees with Nafisa's statement, making Onyinye smile through her tears. She has to know Nafisa is right—she has us, and that's better than a man who can't face responsibility, a man who chooses the easy way out or to flee when things get complicated or don't go as planned. He, whoever he is, doesn't deserve her.

"On the bright side, you get to save so much money on sanitary pads and tampons. You also don't have to go through your uterus shredding every month because there's no baby in it and suffer from the painful contraction it causes. But what I really want to know is when do we find out the sex of our baby? Can we have a gender reveal party? Oh my, we are going to be mummies!" I say, trying to lift the mood from gloominess, and it works. Everyone starts laughing, and it brings about excited chatter from the four of us about babies and the things we are going to need to raise our baby right.

Onyinye plans on telling her parents about her pregnant status tomorrow, and we offer to be there when she tells them, but she declines, saying she needs to be able to stand up to her parents by herself, and she would call us after she tells them. But I know we all are going to drive to her place whether she likes it or not.

I'm pulled away to attend to my duties, such as taking obligatory pictures with the various family members I have and wedding guests. I am called to give a speech, which I thankfully give without making a fool of myself—I do not trip or fall once, my voice also stayed steady, and I managed to make my mum and Mr. Saludeen blush as I shared with everyone how I had caught them immediately after he had proposed to her.

I leave the stage to go and check on Jide's parents, who are no longer pretending that they aren't worried. I try my hand at reassuring them like they earlier told me he is a grown man and we will hear from him soon. I ask if they need anything, and they kindly refuse my offer. I excuse myself to go and check on my friends. I need them to reassure me because I am no longer angry, just plain worried because this isn't like Jide at all.

Before I can get there, I am dragged by my aunties towards the dance floor, to dance with my mum and Mr. Saludeen. I move my worries to the back of my mind and put as much energy as I can muster into dancing and sticking on a smile as I get serenaded by people pasting and spraying me with money. The girls arrive, and Nafisa starts helping me put the money in a bag, and I am very thankful for her help.

Jide's parents also come to the dance floor and spray both me and the married couple with money. After a while, when I feel like I have done my part and danced enough, I exit the dance floor, because I no longer have it in me to keep up the charade and pretend that I am anything but fine.

Nafisa is the first person to see that I am very close to losing it and drags me out of the boisterous hall. Once we are outside and away from everything, she hugs me so hard, it takes everything for me not to start crying. She consoles me until I have reasonably calmed down after that she takes my phone from me and tries to call Jide. But his phone is still switched off, and my phone is empty as far as I am concerned because there is still no message from him on it.

Once I feel functional and able to face the crowd again, I dab at my face, not wanting to mess up my beautiful make-up. Nafisa confirms I look gorgeous, and we head back to the party. As we approach our table, I notice that Jide's parents are there, and Onyinyechi is trying to console his mum. I don't know what is going on, but it can't be good news. I feel a huge weight befall me as my whole body becomes too heavy for me, and it seems like forever when I get to the table because dread has consumed every part me.

"Sewa, it's Jide. He has been found. We know where he is."

It is Nnoli who speaks the words I have been waiting to hear all day. She hands me her phone. Her web browser is open, and loaded on it is a popular news site.

The post had been published twenty minutes ago and the headline read,

Self-made Millionaire Jide Harriman, Chairman & Creator of the Druin Empire, was arrested from his mansion in the early hours of today by EFCC

I instantly feel relief that his whereabouts have been disclosed to us, but at the same time, the weight I am carrying has only gotten heavier as my worry for him has increased. I turn to his mum and hug her because if I am this worried about him, I can't imagine how she is feeling now.

CHAPTER THIRTEEN

I and Jide's parents decide not to inform the newlyweds about his arrest, not to bring a damp spell to their beautiful day. Instead, I follow them to wish my mum and stepdad a happy marriage and say their goodbyes while promising to catch up with them at a later date. I excuse myself as I am seeing them off. Thankfully, the newlyweds didn't ask us about Jide's whereabouts because I don't know if I would have been able to not burst into tears in front of my mum.

Once we are outside and at the car park, Jide's father immediately starts making calls while his mum's phone starts going off. I guess the news had spread widely everywhere now. I stay by their side as they get as much information as they can.

My phone starts ringing, and it's an unknown number. My heart starts beating fast as my hope soars, praying it is Jide who is calling me. I nervously pick up the call.

"Hello?"

"Sewa, hi it's Coker."

"Oh, Coker. Hi, I didn't know you had my number."

"Jide gave me in case of emergencies."

"Oh."

"Are you alone right now?"

"No, I am not."

"Okay, that's good, I don't know how—"

"I know, I've seen the news. I'm currently with Jide's parents. We haven't been able to reach him all day, and we are all worried"

"Wow, with his parents. You guys have gotten so serious."

"Yes, we have. Have you heard from him?"

"No, but I have heard from his lawyer. I will send you his lawyer's number also."

"Yes, please do that. I will give it to his parents, too."

"He's okay, don't be so worried. His business got mixed up with some bad people. Don't doubt Jide. He's a good person, okay, and I'm sure he'll talk to you as soon as he can."

"You don't know how much weight you have taken from me with that statement. I know he's a good man. It's the Nigerian authorities I don't trust."

"He's also a smart, well-educated, and extremely rich man, so trust they can't do anything to him and think they can get away with it. His legal team is also bulletproof. The Nigerian authorities don't stand a chance against them."

"I hope you are right."

"I am. I'll call you later to check in. Hang in there."

"Thanks, Coker. I really appreciate your call."

"Just being there for my future sister-in-law. By the way, tell the Harrimans that I said everything will be fine."

"Okay, bye."

I hit the end button and turn to face his parents who are waiting to hear from me. I fill them in with what Coker told me and watch as they relax a little bit, glad that I have good news to share with them. As I am providing them with this new piece of information, my message notification tone rings out. It is Jide's head lawyer's phone number. I share it with his parents, and his dad immediately calls her.

Mrs. Davis, his lawyer, informs us that they are currently out of the state and are at the EFCC headquarters in Abuja. Jide will be released on bail tomorrow, and then, he will get in touch with us.

She assures us again that he is all right and all the charges against him would be cleared and dropped soon as she will ensure it. We tell her to relay our greetings and prayers to Jide, as well as informing him to contact us as soon as he possibly can.

I believe we can all sleep a lot better tonight now, knowing that Jide has things covered already. I say goodbye to the Harrimans, hugging his mum again before they finally enter their car, their driver patiently waiting. I watch them leave, knowing that I have to return back to the party because my girls will be waiting and anxious for me.

As soon as I step back into the hall, I am instantly called by one of my mum's friends to assist with something, and my happy façade immediately goes into place. I manage to escape after seeing to her need and make it back to my table. Once the girls see me, they perk up and give me all their attention, so I reclaim my seat dramatically and also fill them in.

It is clear I am in a better mood than I was previously, but I am also so done with this wedding party. I tell my girls that it's time to go, and they all agree. Mum isn't coming home tonight—she and Mr. Saludeen have booked a suite at Orientals Hotel, so I don't expect to see her anytime soon. I find Demola, and we all go and tell the couple we are leaving.

The newlyweds are happily busting moves on the dance floor, and when we approach them, they can tell we are coming to say goodnight. Mum stops dancing to

Lara T Kareem

hug each of us and tell us thank you for being part of her day before she gives her blessing for us to leave.

Nafisa is meant to be my ride, but Tosin offers to drop us at home, especially since he is also as done as the rest of us with the party. I am pulled into a group hug by my friends before we part ways.

The ride home is silent on my part as I spend it lost in my head while Tosin and Demola talk about whatever it is they are discussing. Until my attention is drawn by the mention of Jide's name from Demola's mouth.

"What?"

"I asked, why didn't Jide come to the wedding party? Are you both fighting, because you have been angry all day."

I am surprised Demola noticed my moodiness. He is more observant than I give him credit for.

"No, Jide and I are doing fine, thank you very much. It's just that he's caught up with some legal issues and won't be around for the time being. It's just unfortunate he couldn't make it to the party."

"Okay. I know when Mummy sees him, she will have a few choice words to say to him."

"That's between Mummy and him."

Once I say that, Demola takes the cue and lets me be. I thank Tosin for dropping us at home, and he waves it aside and declares he's doing what any other brother would do because he is now legally our brother.

The first thing I do is call Jide's parents when I get to my room. I confirm that they got home with no problem, and I thank them again for coming to the party, before wishing them goodnight. After that, I answer a series of calls from my friends and Coker before my phone becomes silent again.

I go through my nightly routine, of cleaning and rehydrating my body, before I settle down for the night.

I pick up my phone and go through the messages Jide and I have sent to each other to cheer me up because I miss him so much. This is the first day since we officially met that I haven't spoken to him, and it makes me so aware of how much our constant attention to each other plays a role in me having a good day. I just hope he is okay and as comfortable as possible while being detained by Nigerian authorities.

I don't know when exactly I fell asleep, but I am glad I did because I had found it so hard to sleep the night before. Despite sleeping late, I can't help but wake up at an early hour, due to my body being used to waking up early for work.

My aunties are staying with us, so I know I can leave the house without worrying about Demola destroying it without any serious authority watching him. I may be worried about my boyfriend, but he's a grown man, and I have to trust he's going to pull through whatever problem that is thrown his way. Today isn't about me— I have to be there for Onyinyechi. We all have to be there for her.

Nnoli and Nafisa arrive at my house a little before eleven a.m. We have been chatting with each other on the group chat, making sure Onyinyechi keeps us in the loop. She plans on telling her parents the news when they get home from church at their Sunday family brunch.

Church ends by eleven a.m., so by twelve p.m., they would have returned to her parents' home and settled down for their meal, so we plan on heading there by one o'clock and hopefully get there to good news from Onyinyechi.

I am a mess who is constantly checking her phone, waiting for a new update on Jide. His parents have not heard anything also, and we are all waiting because Mrs.

Davis hasn't answered any of our calls today. My constant fidgeting and checking my phone has it taken hostage by Nafisa, who says I am not helping myself. She switches off my phone, ignoring my cries of protest.

"I'm going to send a message to Jide's phone, to call me if yours is unavailable because you're with me."

I don't say anything and let her do what she wants to, because I know there is no way I am getting my phone back from her.

It's a little after one p.m. when we get to Onyinyechi's. We came fully prepared to camp outside of her house, with snacks and drinks. Nafisa even brought her laptop in case we felt like watching a movie because we didn't know how long Onyinyechi will be inside for.

Fifteen minutes later, I am listening to Nnoli rave about a new film she recently watched on her recent trip to the cinema when there's a knock on the driver side window. It's Abdul, Onyinyechi's gateman. Nafisa winds down and smiles cheerfully at him. It seems we have been noticed by the Igwes.

"Good afternoon. Madam say, make I tell you, say you na dey come inside."

I start laughing because Onyinyechi knows us so well, and if she's asking for us to come inside, then it has to be good news and her parents aren't acting very drastic because she's pregnant outside of marriage and the guy didn't even stick around. I really hope Onyinyechi is coping and not succumbing to depression. I'm just glad she has a great support system around her because many other women aren't that lucky.

The Igwes are eating at their patio, and we notice that they have also set tablespaces for the three of us. Mrs. Igwe gets up to hug us when we reach the table. We gladly hug her back, before she tells us to take our seats.

We greet Mr. Igwe who smilingly replies us before we focus on Onyinyechi who is doing everything but looking at us.

"Onyinyechi told us I think my girls are coming, but I'm not sure when. And here you are. It's so wonderful how you young ladies have each other's backs. I wish I had friends like you lot when I was growing up."

Clearly, Onyinyechi had told her parents about our baby, and it seems everything was fine. Her mum was looking at us with so much happiness, we all couldn't help but blush a little.

"Onyinyechi, you can't greet us abi? You're feeling so important now because you predicted we would show up," I say to her, but she just rolled her eyes at us, yet her lips formed a small smile.

The Igwes piled us with food until we couldn't eat anymore. Afterwards, Onyinyechi marches us into the deserted downstairs parlour so she can narrate to us how telling her parents she is pregnant went.

"They were in shock. You know, they didn't think their baby girl was having sex, so I think I scarred them permanently. Mummy didn't know what to be. She was disappointed yet also being supportive. I could tell she wasn't expecting me to be pregnant yet since I'm not even married, but she hugged me and said everything will be okay. Daddy wanted to know immediately who the person was and what our plans were, so when I told them I was alone and the guy ran, it cooled their blood, and they asked me what I wanted to do, with Mummy reminding me that since I am a grown woman now, it's my choice and they will stand by me whatever my decision is."

As soon as she finished talking, she burst into tears, and I know she's feeling so relieved because she was worried about how her parents would take the news. But

I had no doubt her parents would stand by her. We all were raised by supportive and understanding parents, even though they were a lot more overbearing and protective when we were growing up, but we saw it for what it was, their love for us.

Nafisa hands her a tissue, and we give her time to collect herself. It's clear that we are all relieved, and nothing can take away the smiles from our faces. Onyinyechi wipes away her tears before she smiles at us, a look full of joy and positivity on her face.

"I guess we are having a baby!" Nnoli and I scream exactly at the same time, making all of us laugh, because it's too much of a coincidence that Nnoli and I shouted the exact same thing at the same time.

CHAPTER FOURTEEN

I never heard from Jide, and I'm not expecting to hear from him anymore. I've gotten calls from his parents and Coker, all being positive and happy to have heard from him, telling me how he's doing fine and he is close to clearing his name and organization, because apparently, his company had been raising red flags because his organization had become a front for money-laundering operations.

His case is one that is being closely followed by a lot of people in the country. Always making the news and with how well put together he is, he has the sympathy of majority of the population, because he had found out before his arrest that his organization was being used for fraudulent activities and was already working with private investigators to provide the proof needed to arrest the people involved, who are already being held in custody.

It's all great and I'm happy for him in that aspect, but I am equally angry with him because he has earned my anger. How can one person go from *I love you* to no sort of communication? I can't figure out why he isn't talking to me but ignoring me. I know this is about him and I should be more considerate, but it's only me he hasn't spoken to, and he is doing an awesome job at making me feel insignificant and unimportant to him. I am his significant other, the one who he claims to be in love with.

My mum finds out about Jide's detainment and rushes home from the hotel for first-hand information. She was worried, but once I reassure her over and over that he is okay, she instantly calms down and proceeds to tell me how she had been stewing on my behalf that he hadn't shown up, but since he has a legit reason for not coming, she also forgives him again on my behalf. She makes me laugh when she says that, and we proceed to gossip with her sisters about how her wedding party was a success and the different antics people had pulled on that day.

On Wednesday, Mr. Saludeen and Mum treat Demola, Tosin, and me to dinner, our first official outing as an extended family. I am a bit sad that they are all leaving on Saturday. I'm going to be the only one around for the rest of the summer break since Tosin also returns back to the country he calls home. I won't admit it to them, but I'm going to miss them.

This week hasn't been for me—it has just been hard, especially with this Jide fiasco. I have been majorly distracted, to the point I missed a deadline at work. I should have finished putting together the graphics for a new book that was being presented at a progress report meeting, but since I hadn't been bringing my A-game to work with all the activities—i.e. the parties—that had been happening in my life, I had fallen a bit behind. I got the worst dressing down of my life to date by Mrs. Anobi, but it woke up the work addict in me, and I've been using work to not thinking about my life problems.

"Look at how pathetic she looks!"

I am surprised to hear Onyinyechi's voice as I step into the lobby when leaving the office for the day. But it's not only Onyinyechi that is waiting for me. Nnoli and Nafisa are also with her, and they are all wearing enthusiastic smiles.

"What are you guys doing here?"

"She's not even thankful we are here. Ungrateful youth, we came to take your moping self out. We are going clubbing!"

I roll my eyes at Nafisa. They are dressed for clubbing, now that I take in their outfits, but I clearly am not, and I also do not feel like going clubbing. Besides, it's past eight p.m. Who goes clubbing before ten p.m. upwards? I wonder which of them came up with this idea.

"We aren't dumb. We know you're not dressed. We were about to come and drag you from your office. We've got you, girl. Now can you go change in your office toilet. Here, I brought wipes and facial wash so you can clean the day's dirt off your face," Nnoli says to me as she hands me the carrier bag she is holding and ushers me in the direction she thinks the toilet is.

I shake my head at their antics but concede to their wish, because I know if I don't, they will just take over and treat me like a petulant child.

Once I am dressed and my face is clean, Nnoli sits me down in the lobby and makes quick work of making up my face. By the time she is done, it is nearing ten p.m. I can't believe that I am still at my office at this time, or the fact that I got ready to go clubbing in it, not even in the privacy of my office.

I feel a lot better once we pile into an Uber we called and Nafisa plugs her phone to the AUX and starts playing lit songs so we can get our clubbing grooves started before we get to the club. We decided to go to *Rumours*, since it's closer to home, rather than going to the island and pick from the variety of options there.

It's not completely packed when we get there, so we are able to score a corner for us to relax comfortably. Onyinyechi is in charge of looking after us since she will be the only one not getting intoxicated. We all order different alcoholic cocktails and a non-alcoholic one for Onyinyechi.

By the time we finish our first round of cocktails, Nnoli is already dancing, and Nafisa gets up to join her before they pull both me and Onyinyechi to join them. We dance for a while before we beckon a waiter and order for more cocktails and asun to eat; I will never turn down the peppered goat meat. Nonetheless, it was a bad combination because the alcohol in our drinks only further inflames our mouths, due to the pepper.

The alcohol is making its effect on us, and soon, we are pulling Onyinyechi with us to the dance floor to dance with the other club goers. It's so liberating and fun that I forget about my worries and just focus on being in the moment and happy, with my wonderful sisters from other mothers.

Two shots of vodka later, I am buzzed and finding everything funny. I am still coherent and aware of my surroundings, but I just feel so free and happy. We are lounging back in our corner and sipping on water and eating more asun, just enjoying each other's company and laughing about anything, when I am interrupted by someone calling my name questioningly. I look towards the person, and it's Lucas, with two other guys I don't recognize.

"Hi, Sewa. It's a surprise to see you here," Lucas says jovially.

I want to roll my eyes at him. What is so surprising about me being in a club? I smile politely at his friends, who he proceeds to introduce to me. I introduce my friends also to them, and I do not miss the unappreciative looks my friends throw at Lucas, but they remain courteous towards him and his friends.

After the introduction, Lucas still hangs around us, like he has more to say, so I look at him fully, urging him to say it already with my eyes. If he thinks I am going to invite him and his friends to our corner, he thought wrong. I'm not the one who ghosted and became childish when the other was not on the same page emotions-wise.

"Sewa, it's so good seeing you. We can catch up. Can I get you anything?"

I could not hold in the laughter that had bubbled up inside me, and I let it all out. He can't be serious. There is no way I am doing any catching up with him.

"It's not necessary, Lucas. I'm good. I'm here with my girls, it's a girls' night out. It's nice meeting you both, and Lucas, send my greetings to Chika," I say, making him know he is being dismissed, but for some reason, he is proving to be stubborn and not taking the hint.

"Chika and I are over."

"That's sad. I hope you find someone else in future who appreciates you."

Once I say that, Lucas' face falls. Did he really believe that I would still be pining for him? Why are some men so full of themselves? You snooze and you lose, that's your luck. He is still staring at me when one of his friends pats him on his back and the other takes his arm and pulls him in a gesture that says *let's leave*. His friends nod politely to us, and they drag him away. Once they are not within our eyesight again, we all start laughing.

We leave the club by two a.m., the three of us that drank a lot more sober than we were some hours ago. Our different Uber drivers are waiting for us by the time we step out of the club which is a dead zone for my network because once I got into the club area, my phone had read no service, so I'd turned it off and kept it safely in my bag, and Nafisa called a ride for me with Sani's Uber account when it was time for us to leave.

I don't need to pay for my trip, due to the fact that Sani's credit card is linked to his account. So that's a nice bonus to the best night or time I've had in general this week. I'm still smiling in front of my gate as I watch the Uber drive off, when I get a mini-attack and watch Jide step down from a black Range Rover I had not noticed and steadily approaches me with a brooding look on his face.

"Where have you been all night, Sewa?"

The irony of his question. He still has the audacity to utter those four words to me. Unbelievable. I am completely speechless because, for the life of me, Jide has truly shocked me.

"What gives you the right to demand that question from me, Jide?"

"I've been trying to reach you since I landed, and your phone has been switched off since. I was so worried something had happened to you, and now you're coming home alone in a cab, at this late and ungodly hour."

"Jide, please stop acting like you really care about my wellbeing. I'm not a baby, and I can take care of myself. Besides, I guess now you know how it feels to be ignored when you're worried out of your mind about someone."

"Don't do that, Sewa."

"Do what? Say the truth? I've been calling and texting you this past week, but not a single word from you. I was the only one you deemed not worthy of your time. I was so worried about you, Jide. How could you do that to me?"

"Sewa—"

"No! Save it. I just can't deal with you right now."

"Sewa, baby, I'm—"

"I'm serious. Do not. You hurt me, I am still hurting. Do not call me baby, do not call me anything. You show up at my home, and you're acting as if you still have the right to be my boyfriend, but you don't. I thought I knew you, but I realize I really don't. Just go. Leave, like you left me before."

"Sewa. I can explain. What are you saying? We aren't over. You know me so well, and I love you."

"I thought I did. But here you are proving me wrong. Did you think you'll come back and waltz back into my life like everything is alright and you didn't do any wrong? Just go. I don't want to see you. I'm not sober, and the little happiness I just managed to find this week, you once again have snatched it from me."

I turn my back on him because he doesn't deserve to see me cry over him. I bang on the compound gate, but the security guard is already there and opens it for me instantly.

"Sewa, I'm sorry. I can explain," is the last thing I hear from him before the security guard closes the gate, thankfully keeping him out of the house and away from me.

CHAPTER FIFTEEN

"Sewa jo o! Oti to, shebi Jide ti wa gbe e, iwo ni o gba fun? Ma su ekun mo, je ka ma lo."

Is this woman for real? Just because I was crying yesterday night over Jide and she happened to see me bawling my eyes out, forced me to tell her the reason why, and comforted me before she went to bed, doesn't mean I am still going to be crying the next day. I might be moping, but that is all.

It's time for them to go to the airport. Now that's a reason to cry, a free holiday on another continent with my family that I had to turn down because I've gotten to the stage in my life which requires me to be a responsible adult who takes charge of her own life.

I honestly don't know why we are leaving for the airport by five-thirty a.m. when their flight is for eight a.m. I swear it's only when my mum is travelling that she takes care to be extraordinarily early. Demola, on the other hand, has slept off in the parlour. I would be a bad sister if I don't give him a proper send-off and scare him awake. You know what they say: no one ever really grows up, and adulting is a scam anyway.

I walk slowly towards him as our mum disappears from my sight. Once I'm within arm's reach, I grab him hard and shake him like his life depends on it as I scream, "Fire, fire, fire! Demola, wake up, we've got to get out!"

I double down in laughter when he jumps up and takes off running towards the exit.

"Sewa! Why are you screaming? Where is the fire!"

Oh, no. I watch my mum frantically look around, and I try very hard to stifle my laughter but end up giggling. I'm about to tell her to not worry when Demola returns, and the look he gives me is one that makes me burst into laughter again. He wants to kill me, I just know it, and I don't care; it was worth it.

"Sewa, why are you behaving like you're seven years old? Do you want me to have a heart attack?"

"Haba, Mummy! You're too healthy and young to get one. Besides, I was just giving Demola his goodbye gift."

"I can see that you're feeling cheerful. Have you and Jide already made up?"

"Oh, my goodness, must Jide be the reason behind my happiness? I chose to be positive, so I am going to be."

"Okay, ma binu. Oya Demola, Sewa, let's be going. Tolu is already downstairs waiting for us," she says, referring to Mr. Saludeen.

I wasn't angry—why did she have to say that?

I haven't put my phone on since I turned it off at the club. Even after Jide saying he had sent me messages, I just didn't want to be bombarded with his calls or messages, if he'd bothered to do that. But now I am ready, no longer under the influence. I think I can properly face anything that Jide throws my way.

I wait as my phone comes on, and once it has fully booted, I'm met with silence, no steady stream of missed notifications filling my phone. Then the endless dings start as my phone finally connects to the Internet and my notifications flood the device. There is something nice about waking up to various pings from different people; it makes me feel cherished and loved.

I ignore Jide's messages because all my girls are mad at me, and they have the right to be. I totally forgot to text them when I got home, and I didn't help my case because I switched off my phone. The messages they sent back and forth in the group chat are very entertaining, going from worried, to threatening to kill me, to what they are going to tell my family, to threatening to kill me again, and also being worried.

I spend the rest of the car trip apologizing to them and grovelling. Once they are no longer angry, I finally tell them why I forgot to text them and why my phone has been switched off. They instantly crucify me for not starting off with that explanation and inform me they would have forgiven me instantly. I knew that, but it's fun begging when you know you have the winning card, or in my case, the perfect explanation.

I have to end my conversation with them because we have arrived at Murtala Muhammad International Airport, but I promise to tell them what happened when I get back home. It's just past six a.m., and the queue is already looking like thirty people long. Since I'm not travelling, my family volunteer me to stand in line as they weigh their bags and get it checked. Fun times! No, not really.

By the time I say goodbye to them, it's already past seven a.m., and I hug my mum for the longest of time. I'm so going to miss her nosey self being all up in my business. Even if I find it annoying, it's also very endearing. My display of affection makes people passing and around us smile, and I am glad I'm sending on positive vibes to the world.

Firstly, I do not have the apartment to myself. One of my mum's closest friend, Aunty Nike, is here to stay until God knows when, and Aunty Jumoke has also not returned to her home, and I know she won't. The apartment has now become their own holiday away from home, which is very unlucky for me because I know these women will have something negative to say about how I live my life now that my mum isn't here and will be sending unnecessary reports to her.

I lock myself in my room after I finish eating my breakfast of scrambled eggs and fried yam, ready to face my friends and narrate the part of my night they missed, via Snapchat group video call.

"Wow, how dare he ask you that question? As if you were the one who ghosted on his ass! I can't believe this."

I nod in agreement with Nnoli, who looks mad on my behalf. Nafisa, on the other hand, is busy snacking on what looks like kilishi and enjoying the dry beef while looking very serious for a Saturday morning.

"Are you going to forgive him, give him a chance to explain himself? He's back and begging, that's good."

I shoot daggers with my eyes at Onyinyechi, who just smiles at me knowingly. Of course I am going to forgive him, but it depends on how good his explanation is. But he needs to grovel and understand that how he treated me was beyond wrong and unjust before I do. So I am going to let him stew a bit, in the pot of boiling water he purposely put himself in.

I don't bother replying her and focus on Nafisa.

"What is up with you, Nafisa? You look so tense, and that kilishi you're eating doesn't seem to be helping."

"I called him. I gave him a dressing down, and he took it like a champ. He knows what he did was wrong, and he told me he would get you back and make it up to you, but he also told me to stay out of both of you's business, and I agree with him a bit. I think I crossed a line, and I'm so sorry, Sewa, I just don't like you hurting. You two will work it out, and no matter your decision, you have my support."

"Seriously, Nafisa! I've not even checked the messages he sent me, and you called him! That's not how the silent treatment works."

"Silent treatment?"

"Yes, like no one from my end talks to him, so he knows how he made me feel. The point is, Nafisa, I love you. I am so lucky to have a woman like you on my side, and I'm glad you chewed him out, but you should have said something to me first. I wouldn't go off on Sani without your permission, you have my word. Thank you, though. So now, can you chill out, it's not the end of the world."

I watch Nafisa's face transform as she has finally thrown the weight she was carrying off her shoulders, and we all smile at each other.

"I love you, ladies," I can't help but tell them. There is so much genuine love in this moment, I wish we were in the same room, so we could form a group hug.

"Girl, just forgive him already and move on with your happy, mushy love life," Onyinyechi proclaims, and we all burst out laughing, until Nnoli breaks it saying, "For real, though. He has to work for it and earn your forgiveness, or else he's going to think he can do something similar or worse and get away with it."

"I know, girl, I got you. Okay, I've resisted long enough. I'm going to end this group call now and read his messages."

"You do that. Later, my loves," Onyinyechi says, and we echo back our goodbyes as we all reach for our end buttons.

Chicks before dicks always. I love my sisterhood with my girls. I am not surprised Nafisa called him—it's something that everyone knows she can do or does; it's just totally her. I love how loyal she has always been to us. Our relationship is the best outside of the love I have for my family, and I'm always going to be thankful that we found each other.

I am both anxious and reluctant to read Jide's messages because I really don't know how it's going to make me feel. Is it going to make me happy, relieved, and less worried, or is it going to make me feel angry, insecure, and heartbroken? What if he is tired of me and came to finally end it with me, but is trying to be a gentleman? No, he's already being an ass-wipe, so no, he can't be a gentleman in my books as of right now.

In the end, I want to read them more than anything, and I can't let fear rule or dictate the way I live my life because I know it's just not the best way to live life to the fullest.

Jide: Sewa

Jide: I'm back and I'm on my way to see you

Jide: I'm at your place now

Jide: Please can you come and see me, or tell the gateman to let me in?

Jide: Sewa, I'm sorry. I know you're mad, but I'm here now. Please stop ignoring me

Jide: I can explain, baby please just give me the chance to in person

Jide: I've been told you aren't at home, where are you?

Jide: I'll come to you, please we need to talk

Jide: Sewa, it's late are you still coming home? Please stay safe

Jide: Baby please talk to me I'm worried, your line isn't reachable

Jide: Baby, I'm sorry

Jide: I love you, please never doubt that

Jide: I never thought there would be a day you would run away from me. I have hit rock bottom and it's my own doing, I want to take the pain and hurt I am causing you right now, please let me

Jide: I never meant to hurt you, please know that I'm going to make it up to, I love you more than anything and I've come to realise that this week. I was wrong and now I'm only trying to right my wrongdoings to you

Jide: I will never stop trying to earn your forgiveness, I'm going to make it up to you, just give me another chance and I'll prove myself worthy of you

Jide: Goodnight, never forget I love you

By the time I'm done reading his texts from when he was waiting for me to after he had seen me, it takes everything in me not to reply him so I could tell him how exactly he wronged me and how there's nothing justifiable about his actions. Pettiness triumphs my heart in this battle, and I decide I'm going to leave him and try my best not to reply any of his calls or messages to my number, treating him how he treated me, icing him out.

CHAPTER SIXTEEN

I walk into my office hung-over. I'm wearing black sunshades to block out too startling lights and to hide my eye bags. On the bright side, I'm faring better than Nnoli and Nafisa. Unlike them, I'm still able to drag myself to work while they are calling in sick today.

I lock myself in my office and wait for my Tylenol to kick in. I have a bottle of coconut water and a takeaway container of fried plantain and eggs Onyinyechi packed for me. God bless her pregnant self because she's turning into our designated caretaker since she can't take any substance that can harm our baby.

Onyinyechi held a sleepover at her apartment. She called it 'the girls' getaway from troubling reality.' No phones allowed, no contacting people from the outside world, so as soon as we stepped into her home, we all had to send texts to and call anyone who would try to reach us and tell them we won't be available until the next day.

On the day's agenda was binge watching YouTube Nigerian series, *Skinny Girl in Transit* and *This is It*. Eating—one thing I love about Onyinyechi's place is how it's always stocked with the good foods and snacks and grown-up sleepover games, which is just the 18+ version of average sleepover games, which involves a lot of drinking, hence the major hangover all we non-pregnant girls have this morning.

There's a knock on my office door. I groan inwardly and tell whoever it is that the door is open as I turn on my work system. Might as well look like I'm being productive instead of nursing a headache.

It's James, the secretary of my department, and he is wearing a ridiculous cheerful smile for a Monday morning. He enters my office fully and deposits the package he is carrying on my desk. A wide rectangle box, an envelope, and a single red rose. He stays watching me, obviously fishing for information, but once I thank him and didn't say anything else or move to acknowledge the package, he thankfully left my office.

In the box sat delicious-looking cupcakes that spelt "I'm sorry" and in the envelope was a card that simply read '*With all my love, Jide.*' I took a picture of the gifts and sent it to the girls, who found it cute and a sweet gesture, but he's not going to buy my forgiveness with food; he can do better. I carry the cupcakes along with me to our weekly departmental meetings on Mondays to share with everyone in the department, so at least they can have a sweet start to this work week.

By noon, I'm fully functional again, and the rest of my work day goes well. Jide still messages me, but he doesn't expect a response because he just sends cheesy messages to my phone to let me know he's thinking about me, and he has finally stopped calling me.

I leave my office early today because I am in need of a good night's rest and sleep. Because I'm leaving early, I don't need to use public transport to get home, since I can leave with Dieko. I can't wait to buy myself a car. We are heading to his car when a man approaches us, his gaze directly on me and smiling tentatively at me.

"Ms. Adesewa Adedotun?"

"Yes, this is she. How can I help you?"

"Good evening. miss, I am Dupe Kingston. I have been hired as your driver."

I look at Dupe Kingston, who couldn't be that much older than I am, expecting him to burst out laughing, because how can I have a driver when I do not own a car?

"Is this meant to be a joke? It sure is funny because I do not own a car."

"Yes, miss, I was hired by Mr. Jide Harriman, and he has provided a car for you."

Of course, Jide. My estranged rich boyfriend. This is something he can do. Is this his elaborate ploy to win me back? Entice me with sparkling and shining things? It is shocking that he would go this far to make me comfortable, and I guess it's because he doesn't like me riding in cars of strangers, especially if I'm intoxicated and out of it. But a chauffeur for wherever I'm going is too much.

"Okay, you can go back to him and tell him the car and your services won't be needed. I'm sorry to have wasted your time."

Dieko stays by my side not saying anything, but I can tell he is highly entertained by the exchange that is going on between Dupe and myself.

"Please, he told me if I do not drive you today, I won't be getting paid, and I've waited for you all day. I first went to your home to pick you up, but I later found out you weren't around, so I came here instead to take you home or where you want to go after work. I really need this job as it pays well, miss."

He has me there—he needs a job in this brutal economy that hasn't been fair to everyone. Here is an opportunity to assist a young person like me, looking to earn through an honest way. Do I really want to put him out of a job he must have been thankful to have gotten?

"Fine, but how do I know Jide sent you and you're not here to kidnap me?"

"You can call him, miss."

"No, that is not an option. We are not on speaking terms, and please, for the love of everything good, call me by my name, Sewa."

Dupe looks at me and smiles genuinely for the first time. I guess he had been wondering what kind of woman he would be driving around, if I am nice, wicked, old or young, etc. I hope I've passed his test as an okay person.

"Okay, thank you, Sewa. What if I call him and you hear our conversation?"

"I can concede to that."

Jide picks up immediately, and we all listen to him tell me he is the one who got me a driver and provided a car for me. He also goes on about how Dupe is an able and good young man and driver for me. He tries to talk to me, but that's when I tell Dupe to end the call.

I turn to Dieko, who is laughing and smiling. He bids me goodnight and heads towards his own car since he can see that I've clearly gotten my ride covered. I follow Dupe to the car he's driving, and all I know it's a nice-looking Lexus. I get into the front seat, but Dupe insists I sit in the back before he starts driving.

Once I get home, Dupe hands me the car keys, but I refuse to collect them and tell him to take it back to its owner. There's no way I'm going to be held responsible for an expensive car like this if anything bad happens to it.

I don't allow myself do anything. As soon as I am out of the car, I immediately group-call my girls and give them the latest development in Jide's attempt to win my forgiveness. For some reason, they are all rooting for him now and tell me to keep them posted, because of how my love life is becoming fiction-like.

The next day, when I step out of my home, Dupe and the Lexus are waiting for me. At work, I get a delivery again, a big white box with a red bow on top of it, along with another red rose and an envelope. In the box are signed copies of all of Chimamanda Ngozi Adichie's books. I once told him about how much of an inspiration she is to me and how much I love her writing, and now, here he is gifting me with her books that have been signed and touched by her. In the envelope was a card again which held the message *'There's nothing I wouldn't do to make you happy. You're my one and only. Jide.'* My heart fills up with happiness, and I immediately want to call him but settle instead with sending him a text. *'I love this, thank you.'*

And so it began, Dupe driving me to and from work, with gifts from Jide being delivered daily to me in my office. The girls soaked everything I relayed to them like a sponge and were always giddy for more. In fact, James and Dieko started teasing me daily to find out what presents I received on each day. On Wednesday, a wrapped rectangle-shaped parcel with a red bow, an envelope, and single rose arrived, and when I unwrapped the parcel, I called Jide immediately, but he didn't even pick up my call and ignored my messages where I was begging him to stop with the extravagant gifts and I was ready to speak to him now and hear him out.

He got me an iPad Pro, a ridiculous and too-much gift, a wonderful gadget, but just too much. I can't even use the excuse of a holiday or special occasion for receiving the gifts. He didn't need to spend more money on me; I had forgiven him. In the card from the envelope, his message read *'Your wings will take you to passionate new heights. Love, Jide'*

Later that evening, he messaged me and apologized for not being available, caught up in his business and sorting out the issues his trouble with the law enforcement of the country had caused for his organization. He told me he wasn't done, and I would know when he would be, encouraging me to accept and enjoy his gifts because I deserved to be cherished with love and showered with the little tokens he sent and would send to me because it didn't cost him anything to make me happy.

On my way to work on Thursday, my mum called me, which surprised me, and I picked up immediately, happy to talk to her whenever I could. But the first thing she said had me laughing out loud.

"Omo mi, forgive Jide o. That man is a good man. He has called me every day to check on me and has promised to look after you while I'm not there when you let him back into your life."

"Mummy, no good morning to me. What has Jide done? Hope all is well over there? How's Demola and your husband?"

"Everyone is fine o, they are still sleeping. I wanted to catch you before you got to work, so I woke up early. I just wanted you to know that Jide's a good man. There's something about him that just makes me know it. You and I know all too well that there are men out there who are bad but hiding behind a good façade, men who are good but can't help but be terrible people. But I believe Jide is good, inside and out, and we are all humans. We all make mistakes and have our flaws because we can't be perfect."

"I know that, Mummy, I know. I love Jide. Have you heard, I have forgiven him, but he is still on a high with his apology, he doesn't think I should forgive him yet, so he isn't accepting my forgiveness. So Mummy, it's not my fault o. I don't know what he is telling you, but it's not my fault."

"Okay, I'm happy for you. All I want is for my children to be happy as I am right now and not fall into the hands of wicked people. I pray for you all every day, Nafisa, Tosin, Sani, Nnoli, Onyinyechi, Jide, you, and your brother. I care about you all, and it will bring me nothing but joy that you all live a happy life."

"We, too, Mummy. I love you! I have gotten to work now, talk when next we can."

"Okay o, Sewa, my daughter. I love you, too. Have a wonderful day, and don't forget Jide is a good man."

She ended the call before I could have said anything more, putting a non-wavering smile on my face as I head into work for the day. Jide outdid himself this time around because he got me a customized gold necklace, with my name Sewa spelt out in tiny diamonds as the pendant. It brought tears to my eyes because I had never held diamonds in my hands, not to talk about owning a necklace or any jewellery with real diamonds. I would cherish all the gifts he had sent to me this week, and all I wanted now was to hug and see him in order to work out all our problems. The necklace came with a single red rose and an envelope, as well. The card in the envelope read *'You shine the brightest and light up my world. I love you, Jide.'*

Friday finally comes, and I am more than anxious to get to the office and see what Jide sends my way. I've somewhat become used to receiving something from him each day of this week, and hopefully, I can get to finally see him again tomorrow when we both don't have work. I'm tired of him avoiding me and I've told him so, but he tells me to be patient, as good things come to those who wait. I am over waiting and as soon as work ends, if he's still about his bogus patience, I am going to his place and demanding his presence.

I enter my office, and it's filled with roses. Roses are everywhere in vases of all sizes and colours. The scent of the flowers and the sight of them in my office is overwhelming to all my senses and emotions. My heart feels like it's going to beat itself out of my chest as I spot on my desk a single red rose and an envelope, which I immediately rush for an open.

'Please grace me with your elegant and beautiful presence tonight. Yours, Jide.'

CHAPTER SEVENTEEN

I half-expect to see Jide waiting for me after work, but I am met by Dupe, who informs me Jide had already instructed him to take me home so I could freshen myself up and change into more comfortable clothes before Dupe took me to him.

I don't know why I am surprised by this because it has always been clear Jide is the kind of person that can be extra to the max, a person who would go the extra mile to prove his point in all ways, and I guess it's one of his attributes which makes him so good at what he does.

I am kind of nervous, because I honestly can't help but think of extremely horrendous things that would make Jide not speak to me, things where intense guilt is eating away at him and all the grand gestures I've been getting all week isn't a simple apology, but because what if what he did or has done is something we can't come back from?

I take a long and soothing shower. Afterwards, I have a one-woman dance party with my towel wrapped around my body. Doing that loosens me up and shakes off a lot of my nerves and the anxiety seeing and talking to Jide dredges up in me.

I am going makeup-free because I have a feeling I'm going to end up crying tonight. Besides, he said dress comfortably—I might as well be going to his place. I opt for jeans and a stretch top that has one long sleeve to my wrist and the other is sleeveless. I dress my natural hair stylishly, in a way that it accentuates my face and I look beautiful.

I inform my aunties that I am going to be out late. They just smile at me and nod. They had been curious when they noticed I had a designated car and driver. They didn't hesitate to question me about it, wanting to know how and why, but despite their concerns for my wellbeing, I could tell they were wrongly judging me, and my assumptions were confirmed when my mum called and asked me about it.

When I explained why Jide has given me a driver and car to my mum, she was understanding as I expected, but she also made things awkward and cringe-worthy when she reminded me to be wise and make use of protection if I am sleeping with him. Apparently, my late nights at the office had been misinterpreted to my mum as me staying out for late night rendezvous with a man. Why are old aunties like this?

I'm twenty-three years old, for crying out loud. I am a working woman; I don't have to depend on anyone to pay my bills anymore. I'm old enough to run my own life, and just because I have an active social life doesn't mean or equals to me behaving wayward and even if, what I do or do not do with my boyfriend is nobody's business but ours. It's annoying, their judgement and spying because I am behaving exactly like how I always do, with my mum around or not.

My mum is understanding of my plight and promises to talk to them. She also reminds me that they are elderly, and I shouldn't forget that her sisters are older than she is and aren't that savvy with times, because not everyone can be as cool and as understanding as she is. I kid you not, she said so herself.

I am on my way again one hour and some minutes after I get home. I've got my nerves under control, and

I'm busy doing everything I possibly can to get my mind off Jide. I notice that Dupe isn't driving towards Jide's place, and when I ask him where we are heading to, he informs me he can't answer my question because he has been instructed not to tell me. No matter how I plead and question him, he doesn't answer me.

I am left guessing where we are headed for a while because we get stuck in traffic, and the cherry on top, we get detained by police officers who have no right to stop us, but like every other police officials who are surveying the roads. They stop to harass us, by raiding the car and asking for the particulars of the car and Dupe's driving license, after that, and they don't find anything. They start greeting me, asking me about my day and my whereabouts. I politely answer them and ask them if I can go, when one of the officers typically says, "Anything for the boys?"

I roll my eyes because obviously, this was where they had been heading all along. I reach into my bag and give them a thousand naira note before they thank me and allow me to be on my way again.

I ask Dupe again where we are heading, but he chooses to keep quiet for the rest of the ride and only focuses on the road.

It's a park. I don't know where, but it's a park, I can tell from the parking lot. Dupe tells me to head inside once he parks the car because Jide is there waiting for me. I become nervous all over again, but I pep-talk myself into getting out of the car.

I walk to the entrance where the security guard stationed at the gate smiles welcomingly at me, and I smile back at him as he lets me into the park.

"Ms. Adedotun?"

"Yes, I am she."

"Okay, I was told to give you this and to tell you to follow the petals."

Upon the word petals, I look at the pathway in front of me, and there are red petals on the floor that are beautifully illuminated by the streetlights. My heart melts instantly, and I open the envelope, eager to read the message within and go on the mini-quest to find him. There's no way he's going to end our relationship. All these gestures are romantic in nature; there's no way he's going to blindside me with a break-up.

'*Thank you for coming. The roses will lead you to me, where I eagerly await your presence*'

I follow the petals, and it looks so beautiful, the darkness of night time making the roses stand out more with the streetlights lighting up the pathway. It's not a long walk before I find Jide. What I see is beautiful, and as I feared, my eyes fill up with tears.

It's a candlelit picnic. I don't know if there's an alternative to calling it a picnic 'coz it's at night? There's a huge blanket covering the floor, with electric candles sticking out of the ground all around it. There are throw pillows of all sizes arranged on one corner, and the food also on another corner. Jide is kneeling in the middle, holding a bouquet of roses and an unsure smile on his face as he watches me approach him.

I love this man. I love him because this right here shows me he cares about me, because he took his time to plan and set this up, cherished me with gifts, which pales in comparison to this, because him doing this is much more personal.

He drops the bouquet when he notices the tears flowing from my eyes and gets up to come to me. He hugs me before he helps me in wiping my uncontrollable tears.

"Love, please don't cry. Your crying tears me apart."

"This time, they aren't bad tears. I'm overwhelmed, but in a good way."

He hugs me again, holding onto me longer than he did before. He leads me to the blanket. I remove my shoes and step onto it, and we lie down where the pillows are. He stacks lots of pillows at our backs, so we are also a bit upright.

He crawls until he gets two wine glasses, fills them with ice and gets a bottle of wine, which he places in front of me before returning to fill two plates with sandwiches. He hands one to me before he settles down beside me and pops the cork of the wine bottle, then pours some wine into our glasses.

I start eating because there isn't anything else to do but stare at him, and I'm not sure exactly what I'm meant to say to him yet.

"You really outdid yourself, with all those gifts. I loved them, but they weren't necessary, Jide."

He shrugs at me and looks unapologetic before a smile breaks out on his face.

"It made you happy and put a smile on your face. I would do anything to make you smile or happy. I'm glad you loved them."

"You know you can't always buy your way to earning forgiveness? And you had to do that because you knew you already wiped the smile away from my face and dimmed the lightbulbs that power my happiness, when you ignored me like I had killed your pet."

The smile falls from his face immediately, and a myriad of emotions such as worry, regret, and pain flash on it before it settles on remorse. He drops his plate and wineglass before he gets on his knees and sits on it facing me, and I know he's about to explain.

He knows I'm ready now to hear him out, knows he had given me the time for my anger towards him to simmer down and for me to be reasonable in my actions and response towards his explanation for being brutal and cold to me.

"When I missed your mother's wedding, I felt terrible, like a huge failure when it came to you. Especially with how my detainment made public news on your mother's wedding day. I did not know how to face you and your family. I really beat myself up, because I had now become an embarrassment to you. I started panicking, and the negative thoughts I was having about us continued to build, and I started doubting what we had because I got scared your mother would tell you to cut ties with me, so you would not to get implicated or further entangled with my mess and whatnot."

"Really, Jide? My mum? When have you ever gotten a judgey vibe from her? She is one of the most understanding people I know, and you know this yourself. We have faith in you, Jide. Those of us who know you know without a doubt that you are not a criminal. I was with your parents when the news came, and it was at night. You didn't think to tell your lawyer or whoever to reach us. We were worried sick and trying to hide it because we were at my mum's wedding party."

"I'm sorry. I know your mum is anything but wonderful. She is an amazing woman, but you have to understand I wasn't thinking straight, and in my head, all my actions were justified because of the thoughts doubting us had me thinking and believing. It's really hard to shake negativity once it sets."

Hearing his explanation makes my blood boil because all I'm hearing are excuses for there is no way my mum and I would abandon him because of mere allegations. We would have fought for him and done everything possible to help, because he's one of the good ones—it's so clear to anyone who meets and bothers to know him. What I really want to know now is why he was having doubts or is having doubts? Because I'm starting to believe he doesn't think I love him.

"I wanted more than anything to hear your voice. To talk to you. But I couldn't because I was scared. I did not want us to end. I was afraid speaking to you would end up with us splitting, and all I knew was I wasn't ready or would ever be ready for you leaving me. It helped that I was working hard to clear my name and organization, so I was highly distracted from my thoughts of you, but it didn't last long, my negativity about us. I missed you more than anything, and the guilt I felt for ignoring you was eating away at me. I was hurting you. and it was stupid because hurting you is only hurting myself, because when you hurt, I hurt."

"You really hurt me, you big old mumu. Jide, I was used to always having you just a text or call away. I love talking to you, the constant attention you shower on me, and how wonderful you make me feel, because you always have had my back, yet you so easily cut me off like that. It was equal to you stabbing me in my chest with a butcher's knife."

"I wanted to talk to you, Sewa, you have to believe me. I knew I was wrong and I had to make it right, but it was already too late by the time I made up my mind because I knew my actions would definitely set in motion the process of you now doubting me and ultimately leaving me. Calling you to apologize and explain everything felt wrong and unjust, I owed you an apology in person, looking you in the face as I begged for your forgiveness. Now I know it was wrong not to talk to you at all. How I treated you was callous, thoughtless, and wrong. I truly am sorry, Adesewa."

"For someone so smart, Jide, you made a grave mistake. You should have called, texted, or emailed me. Whatever! You should have reached out to me, period. I doubted us because you made me. I thought it was over. You were the one who left me out in the cold, not the other way around, and you should know the thought of leaving you makes me ache and it's so unbearable. I was very angry, yes, but I always had hope that we would work things out."

A sad smile is on both our faces, and he reaches out for my hands which I allow him to hold. He drops a kiss on the back of each of my hands before he starts speaking again.

"I doubted us. I got scared, but there's no way I can't be without you. From the moment I saw you again, at *Palm and Co.*, I knew you were important to me, the person to share my future with. I love you like I've never loved anyone else. Give me another chance, and not a day will go by without you knowing the love I have for you is true."

"You're really going for romantic of the year, Jide. You do know I love you, and you never have to doubt I do, right?"

"I know, Sewa, I know. I just panicked, and I'm sorry I put us through our relationship's version of Hell."

"I know, right? You kicked us out of the honeymoon bubble we were in about how we feel about each other. Shame on you!" I laughingly tease him, lightening up the mood and making his smile reach his eyes this time, as I know I had dashed away any fear and restored his faith and hope for our future together, as he had restored mine.

"What are you even saying? Can't you see we are already on the right track back there? This was just a tiny iceberg thinking it could sink our boat, but now, it knows it's no match because our boat is the strongest, and I know it can weather through anything."

My heart is beating so fast because his words move me so much, and my eyes fill with tears again, but they don't fall. I also get on my knees, take his face in my hands, and kiss his lips like I've been dying to for weeks, before hugging him and resting my head on his shoulder.

"That was very sweet and lovely, Jide."

"Marry me."

I push him away and end up falling on my butt as I start laughing. Is he joking right now? I look up at him, and he's looking down at me sheepishly, now with only one knee up, an arm outstretched towards me as he palms an open small box. Inside it, on a cushion winking at me, is a beautiful ring that matches the jewellery set he recently gifted me.

I sigh loudly and close the box before patting the space beside me for him to sit down because there is no way I am going to answer him tonight without crushing his ego and reducing his self-esteem. I have to explain why.

"I love you, Jide. I really do, and I shouldn't be surprised you spring an engagement on me, because of all your recent actions and this extremely romantic setting, but I am."

"Is that a yes or a no? Because I'm starting to feel you're letting me down, gently, and I really appreciate it, Sewa. I never imagined you would laugh like that when I proposed to you."

"Of course I laughed." I can't help but smile now. "We just made up from our first major fight, and even though I hate to think about it, I know there will be more to come. I am also not ready to be married because there are still a lot of things we don't know about each other and are still discovering."

"An engagement doesn't mean marriage, Sewa, I know this. I love you, and I know it's you that I want to spend the rest of my life with."

"And I you, Jide. I just don't think we are at the marrying stage yet. We haven't even seriously discussed marriage and any of the life-changing things marriage brings, so please, can we postpone our engagement indefinitely?" I ask him as I reach for his right hand and hold it in between my palms.

We are staring into each other's eyes, and I can see he's a bit crushed, but he knows there is still hope, because he nods at me and sighs as a slow smile takes over and uplifts the sombre features that had taken hold of his face.

"Okay, Sewa, I concur, but I'm still going to cry to everyone you told me no."

"Oh, please, you will live, and who knows? I might be the one to propose the second time."

"Not if I beat you to it."

"Jide, it's not a competition o!"

I laugh at the devious smile that is now gracing his face. Of course, I am thrilled and happy he proposed to me, and right now in this very moment, I'm the happiest I can be and am so thankful everything in my life has somehow aligned because, for once, everything is moving at a steady and smooth pace in the right direction.

"Love, before we forget ourselves in the presence of each other, let's eat the delicious meal I packed for us. I know the foodie in you will approve," he says before he proceeds to feed me a sandwich, which he stuffs into my mouth once I open it to take a bite and laughs when I glare him.

I really am in love with this beautiful man, and I really pray and hope we spend the rest of our lives together.

CHAPTER EIGHTEEN

Jide is in the good graces of all the females in my life. Once I narrated how he apologized to me and how I turned his marriage proposal down, he went from being the bad person to the good one and I the worst person.

My mum couldn't believe I turned down his marriage proposal. I know she likes him a lot, but she is meant to be on my side, not his, even though in the end, she told me no matter what, she would always support me and I was right in my decision to say no. But every now and then when we talk, she exclaims she can't believe I turned down such an eligible husband candidate. When she does, I have to remind her that it's not that serious because we would eventually get married, but she scoffs when I say this, and I've just learnt to not comment anymore. I think she just does it to tease and rile me up.

My girls couldn't believe I told him no because they were the ones who'd told him to go for it and ask me to marry him. I couldn't believe them, and I gave them an earful when next I saw them in person. Because they didn't consult me at all, they did not even try to find out my views about marriage with Jide, or if I was ready.

I informed them that they were not only bad friends but also bad researchers and informants, which proceeded to make all four us burst into laughter and kiss and make up. At least now, if my boyfriend or their future boyfriends, fiancés, or husbands recruits us for help, we will always find out without giving away clues

Bose ushers us into Mrs. Ehi's office as soon as we step out of the elevator and onto the Human Resources department floor. We exchange morning pleasantries, and I introduce her to Jide before she gladly tells us how right on time we are because Mrs. Ehi had just finished settling down and is now ready to start her workday.

As we get closer to her office door, out of nowhere, I become a nervous wreck because I am feeling like I am reporting to my secondary school's principal's office because I was caught doing something bad.

Jide enters before me and lightly drags me in while silently laughing at me. Mrs. Ehi, who is seated behind her desk, cheerfully gets up and welcomes us—well, mostly Jide into her office before we all take our seats again.

Seeing that Mrs. Ehi obviously has professional respect for Jide, I choose to let him speak on our behalf, and I only speak when I feel it's necessary I do so. Us informing her about our relationship is the right step because she gladly tells us we are the first people within the firm to acknowledge how our relationship could raise red flags if the management isn't aware, and hopes us doing this will also inspire others to take this step in letting HR know about their interwork relationships.

There is paperwork for us to fill and sign, ensuring our relationship won't disturb or affect our professional responsibilities and also be responsible for assuring that our relationship does not raise concerns about sexual harassment, favouritism, sexual discrimination, bias, ethics, and conflict of interest.

We leave her office smiling and holding hands. Bose grins and signals her thumbs up at us as we pass her desk on our way to the elevator. It's almost eleven thirty a.m., and the conference doesn't start until noon. Instead of heading down to the event hall to get settled in before the conference starts, we head to my office like we are secondary school teenagers, looking for a way to while away time and be alone with each other, even if it's only for some few minutes because this is our only chance for privacy for the rest of the day at the firm.

Today, my firm announced it has secured the publishing rights for the franchise that is the Viola Trilogy by Tessa Monaé in the whole of Africa. Not just West Africa or South Africa, but Africa the continent.

I am still in shock. Never would I have dreamt or thought that there would come a time where I would get the opportunity to work on or create graphics for and have my name attached to such a prestigious project.

I am going to meet *the* Tessa Monaé, one of the women I look up to and whose success constantly reminds me that I can achieve great things, too. And I am going to be part of the graphic design team for her books—she is going to know me. As soon as I heard the announcement and my brain started calculating what it would mean, Dieko and I immediately started hyperventilating, because both of us surely just discovered what it feels like to enter, be acknowledged, and accepted in fangirl Heaven. And when Tessa Monaé stepped onto the raised platform herself, I think my heart stopped for a second before it started working overtime and my body started to shake with the rush of emotions I was feeling. I didn't even know I was crying until Dieko handed me his handkerchief to wipe my eyes.

No matter what now, working on this book is going to boost my résumé by miles. It will give me a reputation that only a few people can claim to have, and it also means we as a team have to bust our minds and brainstorm to create the most epic book covers and inner graphics this trilogy has ever had. The pressure is real, and I love it.

The conference ended a bit after five p.m., and we were free to go home after and start the weekend on a happy note. All through the ride home, I can't help but only gush and speak about Tessa Monaé, and Jide is more than thrilled because he just keeps on smiling endearingly at me. I guess it is because he has never seen me in full-out fangirl mode.

Immediately as I get home, parting from Jide is hard, because I feel like I'm leaving behind a part of me I need to function properly, and if I am being true to myself, I want to spend time with him instead of going out with the girls. I'm about a minute from cancelling with them and going over to his place in order for me to get even more lost in everything that is Jide.

Even though I know if I cancelled on them they would understand, it would not stop them from rubbing me not going to the concert in my face. Besides, a night out with the girls is always a good time, and it would be fun dancing and singing live to our favourite Nigerian artists. I have been anticipating seeing and listening to Lady Donli performing live because I've been to other concerts in the past and have seen many other artists perform, but not her yet, and going tonight would change that and make me a permanent member of fangirl Heaven today.

From the concert, we'll be going to Jide's place, and Dupe has agreed to drive us to and from the show, so he's going, as well. Jide didn't want to come because it is a girls' night out, and he's better off without being in a confined area with hundreds of people and loud noises, including the music. Because I know we would leave the concert late, everyone including Dupe will also be sleeping at Jide's place. Jide gladly accepted our conclusion because he now refuses to let me be out late without a car or someone he trusts to drive me back home.

I love dressing up for concerts because it's so easy to dress for. Nothing too fancy, and the more stylishly comfortable, the better. The first person to arrive is Onyinyechi, and she helps me with applying makeup to my face as we talk about life in general. I am waiting for everyone to arrive before I start gushing about Tessa Monaé, so they can start complaining and tell me to shut up at the same time, plus I don't want to repeat the news I have to share three times.

Since Dupe is driving us all to the venue, my home is our meeting point. The concert starts at eight p.m., and we leave my home by nine p.m., which means we would get to Eko Hotel around ten p.m. and into the event hall a bit to eleven p.m. if my estimation is right, knowing the later the better, because when it comes to Nigerian concerts, they never start early, especially ones as big as this.

Never have we gone to a concert together and opted for getting ourselves a table, because tables are ridiculously expensive. But seeing as Jide had several tables for being one of the sponsors for the show, there's no way we aren't taking advantage of that.

As we are getting our table entry hand bands, I spot Dieko and excitedly wave him over. I wasn't expecting to see someone from work here, especially not Dieko because we never discussed concerts. I reintroduce him to everyone, just to jug their memories, when I notice that he is wearing a VIP band on his wrist. Our table is for six people, and we are only five, so I ask him if he wants to come stay with us at our table. He doesn't believe me at first, asking me if I am being serious, and when everyone nods that I am, he happily accepts and exchanges his VIP band for a Platinum Band, even joking that from now onwards, he's going to be tagging along with me for shows and events.

We arrive right on time, because not up to five minutes after we are directed to a table near the stage than no other than Lady Donli graces the stage. I'm so excited, I immediately get up and start singing along with her, making my friends do the same, and I look round the hall and see many other people dancing and singing along to her songs.

I notice that Nnoli and Dieko seem to be having a great time talking, and I throw the others a look, which they give me back, telling me without us speaking that they already noticed it, too, and we would discuss it later. One of the best things about our friendship is that we can communicate with each other without speaking words, and it's so beautiful to be connected with them on this level.

By the time we decide to leave, we are so buzzed and we more than enjoyed the show, and we are all tired and can't wait to clean our faces and take a nice bath before we go to bed. I spy Nnoli and Dieko exchanging numbers before we go our separate ways, and I loudly cough, but they both choose to ignore my obvious teasing.

Getting back to the mainland didn't take time at all since it was late and there was zero traffic on the road. I had to make sure everyone was settled in for the night before I made my way to Jide's room.

I knew he would be asleep. He said he would wait up for me, but I told him I wouldn't count on it, and here he is sleeping. As I watch him sleep, my heart is filled with peace and love. There's something soothing about watching him sleep. I quietly go about cleaning my face and taking a quick shower, before I slip into his bed with him.

"Did you enjoy yourself, love?"

I am surprised when I hear his sleepy tone asking me the question. As I settle into the bed, I feel his arm go round my waist and pull me until my back is to his chest.

"I did. It was amazing. You should have been there."

"It's fine. What about your friends and Dupe?"

"They did also, and they are all settled in. I made sure of it before I came to bed."

"That's good. I'm just glad I have you in my arms now."

I wiggle around a bit until I am comfortable and hear him release a soft, sleepy chuckle. I am also sleepy, and any minute now, I'll be in dreamland, so I better tell him now.

"Babe, I am so tired, I'm going to fall asleep any second now, plus you and your bed aren't helping with how good you're both making me feel."

"Alright, goodnight. I love you."

The last thing I remember saying is "I love you, too" as I got lost in the land of sleep.

EPILOGUE

"Look at how cute Anissa is, Jide! It amazes me how big she gets with each month that passes. She'll soon be seven months, and she's looking about nine months."

Sewa leans over, stretching her phone so I can see the picture in question. Anissa is indeed a cute baby. Our goddaughter is one of the cutest babies I've ever seen, but I know whenever it is that Sewa and I have kids, our babies will always be more beautiful and amazing than any other kids. It's a popularly known fact that we both have good genes to bless our children with.

"I don't know why you're surprised. With the way all you ladies treat Anissa, it's a wonder she doesn't look like a toddler."

Ever since Onyinyechi gave birth to Anissa in February, it has become commonplace that Anissa is mentioned in almost every conversation that any of the girls have, and it is even more pronounced when they are all together and Anissa is present. The way they all fight to carry and entertain her makes Onyinyechi and everyone else's heart warm with laughter.

Onyinyechi is always bombarding us all with daily pictures of Anissa, so the girls will always know what's up. It's like the four of them gave birth to Anissa and Onyinyechi was just the person chosen to carry their baby. Ever since Anissa got weaned off her mum's breast milk, the girlfriends all share her, taking her every other day for two days.

Sewa drops her fork and wipes her mouth clean, then checks her handbag. She's looking for her lip balm. I watch her with a smile on my face—she always does this after every meal. It has become our tradition now. Anytime she stays over, we always have breakfast together, and we won't have it any other way. Today had been my turn to prepare breakfast.

Sewa gets up and straightens her outfit. She is looking at her reflection on the fridge's door; she turns left and right before she catches me looking at her. My smile widens. She's so beautiful, and just being in her presence makes my heart swell with love and pride.

"Are you really sure this outfit looks good on me?"

"Babe, everything looks good on you. You wear the outfit, it never wears you."

"Jide, for real, this is my first day as the head Graphic Designer, and I also have a bunch of interns who will be coming in today—they will be looking up to me. I feel like such a fraud."

I roll my eyes at her. It's funny how she can go from being so sure of herself and everything to picking herself apart and putting unnecessary stress on her being.

"We both know you got this. You might walk into a table or trip over nothing, but graphic designing, designing in general, is your domain, and you deserved the promotion. Even Dieko agrees you've accomplished so much in just a year. *Palm and Co.* know what an asset you are and appreciate you."

Nnoli and Dieko are so into each other, it's disgusting to watch, because they are so in everyone's face about their relationship, but it's also endearing because Sewa and I are also in everyone's face about how in love we are with each other. Our friends are constantly telling us to get a room.

I am happy when I see a smile slowly take over her face. She walks towards me, and when she is near, she bends. I lift my head, knowing what is coming next. She wraps her arms around me as she lands a kiss on my lips.

"I love you. What will I do if you're never there to boost my ego?"

"Don't worry, love. You'll never have to find out."

She straightens herself once again and grabs her bag. She kisses me on a cheek this time around and places a hand on the kiss, stroking my skin lightly.

"I'm going to work now. I'm already missing you."

"Not as much as I am right now, my love. If we could get away with locking ourselves away from the world, you know I won't hesitate."

She laughs at my response. I tell her I love her and kiss her this time around before she heads out for work.

Once the gate closes, I take in a huge breath. There's so much that needs to be set up before she returns from work. I am both excited and nervous about asking Sewa to marry me again. Last year, I was serious when I asked her to be my wife, but the timing of my asking was not right, and even though I felt a bit rejected, I knew she was right, and I'm so sure now that she knows how important we both are to one another, and how right it is for the both of us to be together.

I'm lost in thought when my phone starts ringing. I look at the screen and smile at my early morning caller. Ever since Nafisa and Sani got married in April, it's been nonstop hints from Nafisa about Sewa and I tying the knot also, and this time around, she's one hundred percent sure Sewa is ready and going to say yes if I ask her to marry me.

"Good morning, Nafisa."

"'Morning. I hope she has left for work because the girls and I are ready to come and start setting up."

"I still think it's weird we are preparing an engagement party when neither of us has proposed and said yes. Isn't it too much that we are inviting my parents and Sewa's?"

"Jide, it's not the main engagement party. It's more like moral support, and she won't even know we are here. Why are you second-guessing this? Have you changed your mind?"

How is that even possible? I desperately want Sewa to be mine in all ways. I need her to permanently move in with me so we can start building our own family. I want to belong to her as much as she belongs to me.

"No, never. It's just, I don't want her to feel pressured to say yes."

"She's not going to say no. I promise you, she's ready now… she is always talking about her daydreams about both your future together. You know what, just call the food catering people and confirm with them that they arrive on time and the menu is correct. We'll be on our way now."

She ends the call, not waiting for my response. I do as she instructs me and then call the event planner that is setting up my big living room for the mini-engagement party with my parents and our close friends.

I don't think we would need an introduction party, because both our parents are friends and we all happily get along. The unifying of our families went without any hiccups, and more often than not, my parents take Sewa's side over mine, and her mum takes my own side over hers. It's a funny dynamic, but we love it because it reminds us we are one family now.

I know Nafisa will bring Nnoli and Onyinyechi along with her, and wherever Onyinyechi goes, Anissa goes, so I have about two hours before they arrive and the event planner also arrives with the items needed. I decide to go and take a shower and change into comfy but appropriate clothes.

***

"Is that the man of the hour, doing boring office work?"

I'm startled by Coker's voice coming from behind me. I drop the document in my hand and glare at him.

"How did you get in and I didn't know?" I ask him as he settles beside me on my couch.

He ignores me and reaches instead for the document I dropped and starts going through it. I keep looking at him because I know he will break soon.

He drops the document in disgust and levels me with a look that screams pity for me, and it's making me so lost.

"What?"

"How can you be reading a business appraisal on today of all days? You took a day off from work for a reason, and here you are working."

"I don't need your concern. This is how I relax. If you have a problem with it, it's not my business. Very soon now, this place will be brimming with activity, and it's still hours away before I might become the man of the hour, so I'm savouring the calm before the storm."

"First of all, might, really?"

"Sewa does what she wants. If she isn't ready, she isn't ready. As much as I picture her saying yes to my proposal this time around, there is still a probability she will say no. So yes, I'm using the word might."

By the time I finish speaking, Coker is silently laughing, and I roll my eyes at him. He still finds it funny anytime he remembers or is reminded that Sewa once turned down my marriage proposal. I don't even know why he is here.

"Why are you even here now, hmm?"

"Can't I be here for emotional support?"

"No."

It's my turn to laugh, because of how quick the no left my mouth, but to be real—there's no way he's really here to offer emotional support to me.

"Believe it or not, that's why I am here. Plus perks of running your own business, you can take a day off and nobody will question it. But really, you have got to get your mind off work and just enjoy the holiday that today is. 'Coz when Sewa says yes, this is a date you'll always celebrate."

"So what do you say we do now while we wait for the ladies to arrive?"

"Which ladies? This isn't your bachelor party. What is wrong with you, Jide?"

My mouth drops open. What in the world is Coker on this early in the day? I shake my head at him and get up.

"Sewa's best friends, you idiot. They are helping me set up where I am going to ask her to marry me. Get your mind out of the gutter."

"You said ladies. How would I have known which ladies?"

***

I'm so nervous as I wait for Sewa to arrive from work. Everything and everyone is in place. The generator is on because I don't want PHCN messing up my proposal if the power cuts off unexpectedly.

I'm going to propose to the woman of my dreams, the person who I see myself growing old with, someone my respect and love for grows with each second we spend together.

As soon as she enters, I know she'll get a hint about what is about to come because I have turned off all the lights and set up a trail of real candles this time around

156

that are heart-shaped and rose-scented. The trail leads her to where I am waiting for her on a loveseat, in a bright, candle-lit room.

Our guests are locked away in the living room, which thankfully can't be seen from where I am. They are being entertained by Nafisa and being served starters by the catering company I hired.

Dupe texts me as soon as they arrive, and my heartbeat increases by a hundred. The room gets so hot, I want to put out some of the candles I've lit. I hear when she opens the door and as she stifles a gasp.

"Jide ...?"

I hear the surprise and glee as she calls out my name. I am so nervous, and the adrenaline that's pumping in my bloodstream isn't helping me become any calmer.

I listen to the sound her shoes clacking against the tile makes, bringing her closer to me. I get up from the seat, waiting for her to round the corner and enter the room.

"Jide! What is all this? Did I forget an important occasion?" she asks as she walks up to me and hugs me.

I hug her back, and the contact does wonders for my nervous self because it not only calms me down but gives me a boost of confidence.

I pull back and look her in the eye, a smile on my face that matches hers. I don't remove my eyes from hers as I take her hands and slowly lower myself onto one knee so there's no doubt in her mind it is happening.

"Oh my goodness, Jide. Oh my goodness ..."

I nod at her, and she takes her hands away from my clasp and places both of them over her heart.

"On this day last year, I asked you to marry me, and you turned me down, which I don't regret because it gave us more time to get used to each other, and now more than ever, I am sure that you and I are meant to be. I love you, Adesewa Adedotun. So please say you will marry me."

When I finish speaking, I reach into my pocket and present the box with the engagement ring she had unknowingly picked out for herself. Tears start to build up in her eyes, and when she starts lowering herself to the ground, I shake my head and nod for her to sit down on the loveseat. She drags me along with her.

Her tears are falling freely now, and I'm getting so nervous 'coz she hasn't said anything for what seems to be the longest minute of my life.

She starts wiping at her tears, a smile breaking out on her face, one which she is trying hard to hold back. At the start of that, a slow pain starts flaring up in my chest when she takes my hand in hers and reaches for the ring with her other hand.

"Of course I'll marry you, Jide. I want nothing more. My answer is yes. It's just that I already planned to ask you. I have my ring picked out, and I was going to ask you tomorrow."

"You were going to propose to me?"

"Yes! It would have made you so happy and made up for me saying no to you the first time. I'm the happiest when you're happy."

The pain disappears as soon as it started. I watch her slide the ring onto her finger, and that's when I start to cry. Tears of joy that I can't help. The joy I'm feeling is too much for me to contain. I grab her by the face and kiss her with everything I am feeling.

When we break away, we are both laughing and crying. She reaches out to me and hugs me. I will never stop loving her.

After what feels like forever, we break apart, and I get up, putting out a hand for her to take. She takes my hand, but she doesn't get up. Instead, she drags me to sit down beside her.

I oblige her because right now, I don't really feel like being surrounded by people. I just want to soak up being in her presence and us being alone with each other.

She reaches into her bag and brings out a tiny box which she hands over to me, with a blush and happy smile on her face.

"I love you. I want to spend the rest of my lifetime with you. Will you marry me, Jide?"

Inside the box is the ring she has picked for me. I take it out and wear it.

"Yes. Sewa, I'll marry you."

She laughs and kisses me. I let her. and when things are getting really heated, she breaks away from me and gets up. She puts her hand out for me to take, and once I stand up, she starts leading us out of the room.

"Sewa, where are we going?"

She has a mischievous twinkle in her eyes. and I know why when she laughing says,

"To tell everyone the good news. They are all here, right?"

OTHER BOOKS BY LOVE AFRICA PRESS

Fine Wine by Emem Bassey

Her Golden Eyes by Holly March

Be My Valentine: Volume Two featuring Glory Abah, Rosemary Okafor, Zee Monodee, Mukami Ngari

Revelations by Lauri Kubuitsile

A Little Bit of Love's Magic by Bambo Deen

CONNECT WITH US

Facebook.com/LoveAfricaPress

Twitter.com/LoveAfricaPress

Instagram.com/LoveAfricaPress

www.loveafricapress.com

LOVE AFRICA
PRESS
African Love Stories

www.ingramcontent.com/pod-product-compliance
Lightning Source LLC
Chambersburg PA
CBHW021055130626
46552CB00005B/2113